## *"I'm leaving in a week."*

A week wasn't a good enough reason to jump into bed with the first good-looking billionaire who swept her off her feet. Chemistry or no chemistry, sleeping with Faisal would be a stupid and dangerous move. Stupid because there was no chance it would become a meaningful relationship, and dangerous for the very same reason.

She backed away, her shaking hands giving up on untying her apron.

Abandoning the kitchen, she hightailed it to her room and didn't look back until she closed her door.

She counted the seconds that lapsed from the time she left him.

When no knock came from the other side and no footsteps sounded down the hall, she pressed a hand to her thumping heart and analyzed what had happened downstairs with Faisal.

He'd kissed her.

Correction—they had kissed.

Dear Reader,

I started writing *Temptation in Istanbul* three years ago when I wanted to escape with one of my favorite trope mashups: single dad meets nanny. And that was my first spark of inspiration for Maryan and Faisal's story.

She travels to Istanbul to deliver custody of his young daughter to him, and it's supposed to be a short stay, free of romantic entanglements and temptations, but one thing leads to another... Of course, like most love stories, they have their obstacles to surmount and personal battles to conquer along the way.

It's also set in sublime Istanbul, Turkey! Researching the landmarks and touristy spots was such a joy and a good opportunity for me to plan my next trip now that pandemic lockdowns aren't so restrictive.

I hope you're safe wherever you are and that Maryan and Faisal's romance whisks you away on an armchair adventure of your own.

Wishing you a happy read,

*Hana* xx

# *Temptation in Istanbul*

—

## *Hana Sheik*

HARLEQUIN

*Romance*

Recycling programs for this product may not exist in your area.

ISBN-13: 978-1-335-40714-6

Temptation in Istanbul

Copyright © 2022 by Muna Sheik

For questions and comments about the quality of this book, please contact us at CustomerService@Harlequin.com.

Harlequin Enterprises ULC
22 Adelaide St. West, 41st Floor
Toronto, Ontario M5H 4E3, Canada
www.Harlequin.com

Printed in U.S.A.

**Hana Sheik** falls in love every day reading her favorite romances and writing her own happily-ever-afters. She's worked various jobs—but never for very long because she's always wanted to be a romance author. Now she gets to happily live that dream. Born in Somalia, she moved to Ottawa, Canada, at a very young age and still resides there with her family.

### Books by Hana Sheik

### Harlequin Romance

*Second Chance to Wear His Ring*

Visit the Author Profile page at Harlequin.com.

For my mom and dad, and my sisters.
Love you all, always and forever.

# CHAPTER ONE

"WHAT DO YOU MEAN, the nanny won't leave the airport?"

Faisal Umar shrugged his suit coat on, Bluetooth in his ear, and his fast strides carried him out the door of his office. He was running late, he knew that. Though now he had his head of security and trustworthy friend Burak reporting that his effort to get out of his office building might be *too* late.

"She's refusing to leave. Says that she expected you'd be here, in my place," Burak explained.

Faisal scowled as he passed through the reception area of his office. His capable executive assistant, Rukiya, sprang out of her chair, but a curt shake of his head dismissed her services. As much as he appreciated her work, he was aware she had a full schedule of tasks and milestones for him to complete. He could take the lift by himself. Use that fraction of time to take a much-needed pause. And he asked for any meetings and calls to be put on the back burner while he handled this latest task on his unending to-do list.

Pushing the button for the lift doors to close, he said to Burak, "But you told her that the time and place of the meeting has changed. That I got caught up with work."

*That I hadn't purposely stayed shut up in my office all day.*

"She doesn't care."

Cursing softly, he dragged a hand through his thick curls. It was one problem after another. He couldn't catch a break. "Okay, I'll be there shortly."

Burak didn't mask his surprise. "You're actually coming?"

What choice did he have? The nanny had his seven-year-old daughter, Zara, with her. Zara was coming to live with him now that he had full custody. Her mother and his model-actress ex, Salma, had called him a few weeks earlier from her opulent multilevel mansion in Los Angeles with an ultimatum. Either he took Zara in, or she would be sent to live with Salma's parents in the Netherlands. And though he had no problems with Salma's family, it hadn't sat well with him that anyone else should raise her. He was her father, after all. Wasn't it his duty to step in?

Besides, Zara and Salma had lived with him for the first three years of Zara's life. His little girl had been born in Istanbul. It wasn't like this was his first time parenting.

*Just my first time doing it alone.*

Faisal shook off the icy doubt shadowing that thought and said, "Give me half an hour," before ending the call.

As he tipped his head back to watch the numbers close in on the ground floor, he allowed his thoughts to meander back to his office. The workload that would be waiting for him later caused a shudder to run through him. He couldn't quash the fear that was roiling through his stomach. Months of planning and weeks of wooing a potential partner in the natural gas and oil industry. To finally see the finish line blasted off any lingering hesitation that his hard work might have been for naught.

All he'd wanted was to take his billion-dollar venture capitalist firm, Umar Capital Group, to the next level. But to give back *and* do that?

*A dream come true*, he thought with hope burgeoning in his thundering heart.

If all went according to plan, he would be partnering with this Turkish natural gas and oil company and bringing them much-needed investment. And in turn he secured the promise to helm the largest offshore development in the Indian Ocean, off the coast of oil-rich Somalia. His home long ago.

Even thinking of his plans now roused a smile.

He'd actually be helping boost Somalia's economy, particularly for the people who needed it the most: impoverished families. Building an offshore rig would do that. Real jobs that would offer training, livable wages and transferable skills into other industries. New export opportunities, more fundamental import of food and medications, tourism and infrastructure. The beneficial effect was what refueled his passion on his worst and most trying days.

*But now it's almost here.*

By tomorrow afternoon, to be precise.

The elevator came to a halt, and the doors opened on the lobby. Outside his office building, the cloudless blue skies and blinding white sunlight promised a good day. A hopeful one.

"To the airport," he said to his driver before ducking into the back of his Maybach.

*Everything will be fine. I have to believe it will be.*

Just as he believed this meeting with Zara's nanny would be like nothing he had ever experienced.

"Mr. Umar left the office and will be here soon."

Maryan turned to the brawny, tall man standing over her, his lightly accented English reminding her she'd flown thousands of miles to

Istanbul. He had introduced himself as Burak, head of security for the Umar Capital Group. There were three other men with him, and they all wore the same dark clothing, earpieces and shades to mask their eyes. Anyone who glanced at them knew they were security detail. Their attempt to blend in failed.

Even Zara leaned in at one point and whispered, loudly, "Why are they here?"

Maryan didn't know how to answer her seven-year-old charge.

She eyed the broad-shouldered Burak, and she had to guess he was looking at them, too. She couldn't tell with his sunglasses blocking his eyes. Unsettled but not feeling as though she should be worried about Zara's safety or her own, she wrapped an arm around the little girl's shoulders and hugged her to her side.

They waited on Zara's father.

*Faisal Umar.*

The multibillionaire CEO known throughout Europe and Asia for his playboy antics. It turned out he was a workaholic as well. Not that the media ever focused on that. Too boring. Why report about him working long hours when the world could gab about his fast and furious lifestyle in VIP clubs and on massive super yachts?

She had met him a few times, but it hadn't been enough to judge his character.

Maryan had taken a fine-tooth comb to his background on the plane. Poring over every detail she could learn about him. Adding it to what Zara's mom, Salma, had told her. So far Maryan knew Zara was born in Istanbul, and Salma and Faisal co-parented for a few years. Then Salma landed her first leading movie role and moved to Hollywood to be closer to the heart of the star-studded action.

It did feel a little wrong digging into his background. But she couldn't afford to feel ashamed. Zara would be living with her father now, but Maryan had been her primary caregiver for four years. Naturally, she was concerned. And her concerns encouraged her snooping.

Zara needed a parent who would be present. Maybe not always, but enough that she shouldn't have to feel like a burden.

And as far as first impressions went, Faisal wasn't giving a good one.

She had anticipated he would be there to greet them when their plane landed. Instead, his security goons had swarmed them. They would've whisked them off to meet Faisal wherever he was, but Maryan was fatigued from the flight and mightily annoyed that Faisal hadn't shown up. Putting her foot down had been too easy. She wouldn't budge with Zara, she'd explained to Burak. Not until Zara's dad put in an appearance. She wasn't asking Faisal to bid his company away. And yet that was how his security had treated her demand. Coolly appalled by her request, Burak had turned away to phone his boss.

Luckily, Faisal saw it differently.

Now he had only to show his face and they could be off.

*But what if he's a brute? What if it's clear that Zara won't be safe with him?*

Then she'd have to cross that bridge when they came to it.

"How long do we have to wait here?" Zara tugged on Maryan's hand, her tiny palm sticky with sweat. "Is my daddy coming?"

*He'd better be.*

Out loud Maryan said, "Not much longer, hopefully," and she eyed Burak while she said it to make the point clear.

Zara lowered her head. "Does Daddy not want me?"

Her heart seized painfully at the warble of unease in Zara's small voice. Dropping to a crouch before her, she took Zara's hands and squeezed comfort into her. Without needing to think it over, she assured her, "Of course he wants you. You're here, aren't you?"

"But he's not here," the little girl rejoined with the most plaintive of whines.

"That's because he's a very busy man. Sometimes when adults have to work, they forget the time, but they don't forget their love for family."

Zara nodded, but she looked glum even after, and Maryan's heart broke ten times over.

Finally, when she couldn't take the torture of watching Zara's downheartedness, she left her to stalk over to Burak. Steam must have been misting out of her ears, because she could've sworn he drew up to his full height. As though she posed him *actual* danger. Mentally rolling her eyes, she marched his way. She didn't reach him before a knock on the pocket doors to the VIP room turned all their heads.

Burak scowled and signaled for the others to draw in. They fell into a tactical maneuver, one they must have practiced many times judging by how quickly and efficiently they moved as one unit and one team.

Meanwhile, Maryan retraced her steps to Zara.

"What's happening?" Zara whispered, hugging Maryan and leaning into her.

She wasn't given the chance to smooth over Zara's fear.

Burak opened one of the sliding doors and disappeared through. A few slow and tugging heartbeats later, he returned with someone else.

Maryan recognized Faisal instantly.

So did Zara.

"Daddy!" She shot up from her chair and bounced eagerly, her excitement unmistakable.

Faisal broke off from chatting with Burak, a wide and brilliant smile breaking over his ruggedly handsome face.

He dropped down to a knee and opened his arms to Zara.

Zara looked up at Maryan, her eyes asking if she could go to him. She wasn't about to stop the father-daughter moment from happening. She had her qualms about Faisal, true. And at some point she planned to bring them to his attention. But there was a time and place for everything. Here and now wasn't it.

With a smile and a nod, Maryan gave her blessing.

Zara beamed and didn't wait for any other confirmation.

"Daddy," she squealed, and ran to him.

Faisal caught her, laughing and pretending that Zara had the strength to topple him.

"Zara," he breathed into her hair, hugging her close. "I missed you."

They remained like that for a long while. Maryan hung back, seeing no reason to interrupt their reunion. It didn't matter that her heart was in knots when Zara clung to her father. Faisal had to disentangle her small hands from the back of his neck to get her to look at him. She strained to hear Zara's whisper, pushing off her heels to lean in and eavesdrop over the dull ringing in her ears.

"I thought you weren't coming," Zara said quietly, her head dropping low. Dejection coming off her in waves. Any joy she had displayed at seeing her dad disappeared.

"I'm sorry. I know I promised to be here when the plane arrived, but I'm here now. And I'm not going anywhere else." He pulled Zara into his arms again. From over Zara's shoulder, he finally looked at Maryan.

She could have sworn his eyes widened a fraction.

And he stared a long time. Too long. To the point of making her squirm, and not with an unpleasant and unwanted feeling.

In reality, his staring couldn't have lasted for more than a few seconds, and yet his gaze seared through her. She hugged her arms around her middle, feeling the oddest sensation of having been branded, which was ridiculous because she didn't know him. She couldn't presume through one look that he would somehow desire her.

Of the handful of times Faisal had come to visit his daughter in Los Angeles, Maryan couldn't recall anything more than pleasantries exchanged between them. It wasn't as though their worlds collided regularly.

He lived and worked in Istanbul and was an excessively wealthy bachelor.

They couldn't be more different.

While she struggled to balance paying off her student debt, her rent and her car loan, he had more money than most people ever saw in their lifetimes. And no matter how close she felt to Zara, she had always known that one day her job as nanny would come to an end. Envy that Faisal had the rest of his life to spend with his daughter coated her thoughts and cooled the flare of attraction warming her lower belly. At least most of it by the time Faisal broke eye contact and concentrated on comforting Zara.

Maryan tightened her arms over her flip-flopping stomach.

Faisal stood and clasped Zara's hand as he walked her back over.

"Are you okay?" Maryan asked, her attention lowering to Zara.

The little girl bobbed her head, but with a sullen air.

She opened her mouth to ask again, her heart stuffed in her throat, when Faisal spoke and redirected her focus.

"Nice to see you again, Maryan. Sorry for arriving late. I've been working through a business deal that's been stealing too much of my time."

She supposed his charmingly sheepish smile was meant to be an apology.

Disappointment dropped like a stone in her stomach and squashed the beginnings of a silly crush on him.

She should have been grateful. Catching feelings for him wasn't on her agenda. Instead of gratitude, she felt empty. Until the anger flooded in, fast and abundant.

It took everything in her to accept his handshake. She exhausted her energy pushing the fiery emotion down and packing it away. *Later*, she vowed. When they were alone, just the two of them, and where she couldn't hurt Zara with any harsh words to Faisal.

"I hope you can forgive me?" he said.

He had made his daughter wait—made her believe that she was forgotten. That she was unwanted and unloved…

She looked down pointedly at Zara and then up again, finding herself no less immune to his thoughtful brown eyes. Those striking gray hairs swimming in with the rest of his long night-colored curls. His flaring Nubian nose, sculpted cheekbones, clean-shaven square jaw, and toowide, too-full smiling mouth.

Maryan swallowed at the first blush of renewed heat coursing through her body, humming a siren song she didn't like at all. Not for one second.

She snatched her hand away before she realized what she'd done.

Faisal lowered his hand slowly, confusion written openly on his face.

Zara piped up then with perfect timing, "I'm hungry."

"Good, because we're having lunch together," Faisal told her, his befuddlement erased and his devastating smile back with a vengeance. "I have everything prepared. We'll leave now and make it in time before traffic plagues the streets."

She held his stare when he looked to her, resisting the urge to glance away or trace her fingers over her palm and the phantom sensation of his larger hand engulfing hers.

"One more thing," he said. "I hope you're both all right with boats."

# CHAPTER TWO

THE NANNY DIDN'T like him.

Faisal got that at the airport after she scalded him with a quiet but fiery look. She hadn't even wanted to touch him. He rubbed his palms together, clammy with sweat. Nerves getting the best of him was uncharacteristic. Sinking back into his leather seat, he turned his head to glimpse his guests behind.

He sat up front with the driver, something he rarely did as he preferred to be chauffeured around.

Now Maryan and Zara replaced him in the back seat. And they had to be the quietest people he'd been around in a very long while.

Given the shaky reunion at the airport, he shouldn't be shocked.

Zara looked out the darkly tinted car window, appearing far smaller in the spacious tan leather seating. A stark image of her downcast face at the airport came to mind. A familiar sinking helplessness tugged on his insides all at once.

He blinked and focused on Maryan.

Like Zara, she gazed out the car window at the glass-and-steel skyscrapers and smattering of mid-rise buildings clustered around the Levent. Istanbul's city and business center. From their speeding position on the freeway, he spied the distinct architecture of his office building. The U-shaped edifice of Umar Capital Group was difficult to miss. And a bit too on the nose. But what kind of billionaire would he be if he didn't sprinkle his ego around once in a while?

"That's my office over there," he announced.

"Which one?" Zara asked and leaned as far into Maryan as her seat belt would allow. "I can't see."

"That one," Maryan said, pointing now too.

"It looks like a big *U*," his daughter assessed.

"*U* for Umar, right?" The nanny fixed him with a level look. Surprisingly with none of the hostility from the airport swimming in the shadows of her eyes.

"Yeah, that's right," he said thickly.

Maryan turned back to his building and the skyline of infrastructure, leaving him with the sense that he'd been dismissed now that she had an answer.

There were two things he had been fast to realize about Maryan: she cared deeply about Zara, and she wasn't the type to hide her feelings.

How did he know this? Because he *knew* people. He had to in his business.

Maryan was only sitting in his car because Zara's mother, Salma, hadn't been able to bring their daughter herself. Her career kept her as occupied as his job did him.

Salma hadn't smothered her skepticism about this arrangement with him, either. Her words flooded back. They were as loud as if she were saying them to him all over again right there and then...

*My mom and dad want Zara. They'll be good to her. They raised me, didn't they?* Salma had inhaled briskly. *But you don't trust them.*

*She's my daughter, too,* he'd said, his thumb and forefinger pinching the bridge of his nose.

He'd been alone in his dark office, the floor completely cleared out for the evening. Not even the cleaners had been around to witness his rising headache and his sorry attempt to squelch it before his temples throbbed. Before his heart ached.

*She's my daughter,* he'd repeated desperately. Not even sure if she was on the other end of the line anymore. He wouldn't be surprised if Salma had hung up on him. She was used to getting her way. It was how Zara ended up with her, halfway across the world.

And way too far from him.

He missed Zara.

Now Salma had dropped this chance to live with and raise his daughter unceremoniously in his lap, and she wanted to snatch that hope away just as suddenly?

*I'm her father. Wouldn't it be natural to want her with me?*

*Then you should have left Turkey and come to live near her!*

Salma's low blow had stung more because she hadn't stopped there.

*Let's be honest with ourselves, Faisal. I struggled to do it on my own these last four years. Truthfully, the wonderful nanny I hired should be taking credit for us both. You know that Zara knows more about her nanny than either of us? She cries whenever Maryan has a sick day, which almost never happens. They've bonded.* A brittle laugh and then, *We haven't been the most attentive of parents. I'm always working and you're... well, I bet you're holed up in your office right now, aren't you?*

He'd tightened his lips and cut his narrowing gaze across his spacious workspace. Though he'd wished he could tell her she was wrong, he hadn't had the heart to lie.

*Yes,* he'd gritted out, frustrated with them both. More cool laughter from Salma. *And you're insisting that Zara be in your care. You let her go once. Why can't you do it again?*

He'd only done that because Salma wouldn't be argued with. She would've taken him to court. Made it a messy and lengthy custody battle. And he'd thought of Zara being put through all that, witnessing her parents fighting over her.

So, Salma was right. He had let his daughter go, but she was twisting his reasoning for it.

He'd sighed heavily. *Does the past matter? I'm more than prepared now.*

Quick as always, she'd lashed out, *But how can you be so sure that you're ready?*

He wanted to answer truthfully now as the bitter memory faded away.

*I'm not sure.*

Like Salma, he was married to his profession. Showing up late at the airport proved that. But by tomorrow he hoped he could answer differently. Once this partnership was actualized with signatures, he would be a freer man.

Maryan would see that.

Which brought him to the second thing about the nanny.

She was…breathtakingly beautiful. *Gorgeous.* Radiant even, as though a golden light were shining under her dark brown skin and illuminating her from the inside out. Her beauty had struck him in the VIP room of the airport, and he hadn't shaken it off. The light hadn't stopped glowing around her, either.

It suffused her in the shadowy interior of his car. A halo around her whole form.

He traced a mental sketch of her facial profile and committed it to memory. The line from her forehead to her upturned nose down to the swell of her mouth and the curve to her small chin. Normal and plain enough features. He had seen inhuman and alien beauty in supermodels like Salma.

Maryan wasn't that. What she had was far, *far* better. That inexplicable extraordinary light of hers swept in and enhanced the little, perhaps inconsequential quirks that were so very clear to him.

How her forehead creased when her eyebrows shot up at something Zara said.

How her nose twitched in time with short spurts of air as she coolly exhaled.

How her lips moved rapidly with speech he tuned out as he focused solely on her.

Glancing back to her eyes, she was watching him now, brow furrowing over them. Slowly, warily.

He looked ahead abruptly. Blushing before he recognized the heat scoring his cheeks for what it was. Embarrassment. Lust. More than a bit of both. His fingers had been tapping out his agitation on the console between him and the driver. Forcing them still, but too late as he caught the curious gaze of his driver.

To his credit the driver said not a word.

"You never answered me about the boats."

Maryan stopped stretching and tugged down the hem of her airy long-sleeved shirt where it rode up her stomach. Faisal hadn't been looking there, but having his eyes on her affected her nonetheless as though he were.

As if it were the two of them out and about the sprawling city. Like on a date.

*We aren't on a date, though.*

"I've never been on one," she confessed. Her home in Santa Monica was close to many beaches, but she never had the chance to experience the Pacific on a sailing craft.

"So, you're not averse to boats," he said with a searching look.

"I wouldn't know."

Zara exited the car and immediately clutched her hand, the touch reminding her of the little girl and her needs.

"I'm hungry," she said meekly, a frown tipping her small pink mouth down.

Shame flooded Maryan. She squeezed Zara's hand and blurted, "Your dad was just telling me all about the delicious food he had prepared." He hadn't been, but she figured now could be a good opportunity to witness another interaction between him and his daughter. Because she'd given his reunion with Zara at the airport another once-over during their thirty-minute car ride. Maybe she had judged him too early.

Everyone was deserving of a second chance, weren't they? One last window to get it right?

She thought of this lunch as his.

*Change my mind. Make me trust you'll be good for Zara.*

"I promise this will be the best lunch you've had." Faisal paused and smiled. "Okay, maybe not the *best* lunch. I don't want to set myself up for failure. But it'll be a unique one."

He led them to the curb and grabbed Zara's free hand. "We'll cross first."

The traffic was steady on both sides of the street. The noise of the lively city coming at them from all directions, much like the sun bearing down over their heads. For mid-May, it felt more like summer. She didn't know if that was unusual or not for Turkey. It was hot even by her standards, and she was hardened by temperatures in the high nineties.

Stinging heat wafted from the paved sidewalk. Sweat frizzed the baby hairs sprouting from her hairline. She had her hair tied up in a ponytail, and yet dampness slickened the nape of her neck.

She was frying. A look at Faisal in his tan slim-fit suit had her wondering how he did it. How did he manage to appear cool, suave *and* incredibly handsome when she felt as messy as she probably looked.

She glanced away when his head turned to her. Last thing she wanted was for him to catch her ogling him.

The cars slowed at one point, and Faisal found a break for them to slip through between bumpers. They emerged on the other side safely and walked the strip of pavement adjacent to the waters of the famed Bosporus strait. She recognized it from online images, although seeing it in person intensified the experience.

"That feels nice," she said of the cool spray of water carried on a breeze. Tilting her head into the momentary respite from the heat, she sighed.

"It's really pretty," Zara commented, awe widening her eyes as she looked around Maryan at the Bosporus.

She had to agree; the sparkling waters of the strait were a breathtaking foreground to the other side of the natural boundary bisecting Istanbul… it'd make for the perfect place for a selfie. Something to post on her social media for her friends and family to enjoy.

Faisal must have read her thoughts, because he asked, "Did you want to stop and take a picture?"

She slowed at his request, the lovely Bosporus forgotten momentarily.

"I can snap it for you." He already had his phone in his hand and waved it. His phone case gleaming like it was made of liquid gold. She noted it was a showy new model of a foldable smartphone. As well as a pricey one, if she recalled correctly. He shook the phone temptingly, that heartbreakingly handsome smile drawing his lips up at the corners.

She nearly agreed to his offer, but then remembered she looked far from photo-ready. She had barely managed to brush her hair and dab on her lightweight concealer to hide the dark crescents under her eyes before the plane landed. Now most of her painstaking work had been undone by unprecedented humidity.

"Can we?" Zara asked with a little gleeful hop.

Maryan stifled a groan. She'd forgotten Zara loved taking photos, camera-ready or not. She blamed Zara's mother. Salma was an internationally renowned model. Not Tyra Banks or Iman levels of well-known, but she was well-traveled and fully booked for the most notable fashion shows. She was an actress now, too. A few small roles in big Hollywood movies featuring A-list stars exploded her film career.

Like her mother, Zara was conditioned to glow in front of a lens. Any lens.

She posed for her dad now, making faces of all sorts. Posh ones, adorable ones and downright silly ones.

It had made Maryan worry in the past. Children could be exploited in the industries that Zara's mother worked in. But right then she knew that a few photos with Zara in front of the one-of-a-kind Bosporus meant something else...

It would be one of the last times she would get to be with Zara like this. In two weeks, she'd no longer be her nanny.

Maryan turned her eyes to the wondrously blue skies. When the lashing heat of tears abated, she blinked, and her gaze alighted on Zara and Faisal. Her heart kicked at the sight of their smiling faces, and at the sound of their bubbling laughter whenever Zara's humorous expressions were unignorable.

*I hope you stay like this forever.*

She didn't know who the prayer was for. Both of them, she decided thoughtfully. She didn't know Faisal as well as she did Zara, but watching him now with her, he looked immeasurably happy.

"Feel free to jump in," he said.

Zara waved for her to join. "Come on, Maryan. It's so much fun!"

She believed it. So why was she hesitating? "I should take the photos," she said softly, swiping her hands down the sides of her legs. Her faded light-wash jeans absorbed evidence of her nerves.

That was when he directed his lens at her and snapped a shot. There was no flash, but she knew he had taken a photo of her. At least one. He assessed his screen quietly until Zara rushed to his side and jumped up to see what he was looking at.

Maryan stood rooted to her spot, her veins running sun-bright hot and fiery cold.

"What do you think?" Faisal murmured, seeking Zara's opinion in the most serious of tones. He held the phone lower for her to view.

Zara studied it with a neutral thinking expression. "I don't know…"

"Is it good enough to keep?" he asked.

Maryan squirmed as they both looked at her now. Trepidation glued her tongue to the roof of her mouth, so she couldn't ask what was wrong. Did she really look as horrible as she imagined?

She blew the breath she was holding when they grinned in unison.

"I like it," Zara said. "But Maryan's always beautiful."

Faisal didn't say anything…but he didn't have to. She saw his silent opinion overtaking his face. A hungering look darkened his brown eyes and softened his lips into parting slightly. Seeing the change in him warmed her from head to toe in a way that the sunlight and summerlike heat of the afternoon would never.

She pretended that her blush was due to Zara's compliment, though.

"Fine, you've convinced me." She palmed her hair in a quick effort to jam any frizzy curls under one of half a dozen black bobby pins and fanned a hand to Zara. "Let's make a memory together."

A memory she fully understood included Faisal.

"Watch your step," Faisal said half an hour later as he steadied Zara on the other side of the walkway and looked back at Maryan on the pier. She wore a similar life jacket to Zara. He had assured her she wouldn't likely need it once aboard, but she insisted. And he realized why when Zara felt more comfortable wearing hers when she saw Maryan was as well.

In solidarity, he strapped into a life jacket, too.

"Your turn," he told her.

She walked the short boarding plank more quickly than Zara and gripped his hands for grounding for less time, but what he saw in her face when she touched him, what he felt blooming inside him, left him rattled for longer than he was used to. That would be the second time she stole a breath from him.

Maryan guided Zara safely up the stairs to the teak deck of the sun lounge. Sunlight washed over the small pool and the lounge chairs circling it.

"Wow! I can see everywhere!" Zara's exclamation rang with more of her innocent awe.

Joining her at the railing, Maryan tipped her head and closed her eyes, her alluring face relaxing.

Faisal stepped up beside her. "I don't get to go sailing as much as I'd like to, but when I do, it makes my day."

She opened her eyes. "I can see why."

"Can I go put my feet in the water?" Zara asked them, losing interest in their conversation as naturally quick as any young child would.

Faisal said, "Yes, but be careful."

Zara skipped for the pool.

"We walk on the boat, Zara," he warned, and she switched to walking slowly and carefully and with a sheepish smile flung over her shoulder at him and Maryan.

"You don't like me," he said evenly, his attention on Zara by the pool. He wanted her out of earshot for what he had to say to her nanny.

"I don't know what you mean," she replied.

"At the airport. I saw it in your eyes."

*And I felt it in your hands.*

He flexed his right fist and clearly remembered

the touch of her…and how he liked it too much. "Though *dislike* might be too strong a word, you *do* have some issue with me."

"I care about Zara." She had her back to a stunning water view of the city he loved deeply. Completely disregarding it to supervise Zara. Because of that he believed what she said.

"And you think I don't. Is that it?"

"You were late," she said instead. She might not have answered his question, yet her nonanswer confirmed his suspicion: she was upset with him.

"I'm aware Salma sprang this custody change on you very last minute," Maryan continued.

"It's affected you, too. You won't be Zara's nanny any longer."

The thought of offering her a job had crossed his mind. Although now there was his attraction to her to navigate.

*If I ask her to stay, will it be for Zara or for me?*

Therein lay his problem. He didn't know whether selfishness motivated the suggestion. It had been a long while since he lived with anyone. Almost as long a time as when he had dated seriously.

"What will you do in two weeks?" he probed gently. Curious as to her plans after she left him and Zara.

"My aunt and uncle own a restaurant, and I'll be helping them more on a full-time basis."

"Somali cuisine?" he asked.

"Mostly," she said with a slow nod and an even slower wistful smile. "I'll miss Zara, of course. It won't be the same without her. That's why I want what's good for her." She pinned him with eyes shuttered to her emotions. A beautiful poker face.

It unnerved him, and yet he knew she waited on him to convince her *he* was good for his daughter. Never one for failing a test, he leaned into her unspoken challenge.

"Do you have kids?"

She scowled immediately. "No, but that wouldn't give me any special authority on the matter. We're not discussing other children; we're talking about Zara. I've been her nanny a while now. That gives me an opinion."

A brisk wind toyed with her curly ponytail, her long black tresses helpless in the gust buffeting the top deck. As helpless as he felt when his fingers itched with a longing to reach out and pull the raven strand plastered to her cheek behind her ear.

He fought against the misleading instinct and said, "I'm asking because I had to know what got under your skin before my tardiness did."

"Excuse me?" she snapped.

Faisal rested fully on the support of the railing.

The boat's motor, now on and running steadily, purred through to his bones. The familiarity of his position calmed him despite delving into deeper and more personal territory.

He'd thrown open the door to it. He couldn't turn back now.

"I thought it might be me. Sometimes I rub people the wrong way before I meet them. They make assumptions about who I am based on my wealth."

She squinted at him and shaded her eyes with a hand. "Are you finished accusing me?"

He shook his head, flabbergasted. "I wasn't—"

"Weren't you though?" She cut him off, her irritation smacking into him like a wall. Hard. "It's true I didn't like that you were late. But that's entirely because Zara had noticed your absence. She…she felt like you didn't care."

Shock turned him into a pillar.

And when he thawed he jerked his head to Zara and watched her with a fast-growing ache in his heart.

*She thought I didn't care?*

"How?" he rasped. *Why?* What had he done to make Zara feel that way? Didn't she know that he loved her unconditionally and endlessly? Hadn't he made that clear enough? And now that he knew he hadn't, how did he go about undoing any damage he'd unknowingly wrought?

He *truly* believed he could be there for his little girl.

Salma's words reverberated through his head. *How can you be so sure that you're ready?*

Swallowing his self-disgust, he asked Maryan, "Is that all?"

His ears had grown hot, and a whining buzz filtered out the lapping waters along the gleaming white hull of his midrange sailing yacht. He swayed in place and shifted to his side with a hand steadying on the rail.

Maryan eyed him. He could've sworn a shadow of regret passed over her face.

"Is that all?" he repeated through gritted teeth.

"It's fine. I told her you were late for good reason. She's young, but she's learned from having lived with her mother why some adults could be busier. Why her parents are, specifically."

She had stood up for him? The nanny *defended* him.

So much for his theory that they had started off on the wrong foot. They *had*, but maybe not as badly as he assumed.

"It's not fair Zara ended up with us for her parents," he said, voice gruff with guilt and shame. The memory of speaking to Salma about this very topic at the edge of his mind. Doubt fisted his poor defenseless heart. "I wanted her to live with me. To do it, I had to get around Salma's plan to send Zara to her grandparents."

Maryan didn't show an ounce of surprise at that news.

"But you knew that because she told you."

"She's a good talker, and I'm a good listener," she offered, a ghost of a smile on her lips.

Faisal returned it with what felt less like a smile and more a grimace as he delved deeper into the sticky, suffocating bog that his fear was growing into.

"As hard as I was fighting for Zara to come live with me, I also could appreciate Salma's doubting my abilities." He hadn't given Salma a reason to place trust in him. It was true, he hadn't striven harder to stop her from taking Zara away the first time. It made him wonder if he'd changed all that much. If he was ready to take on the challenge and reap the rewards of single fatherhood.

"Do you feel like you can't do it?"

Maryan's query centered him in the present. He was there and now with her, and not sinking faster and succumbing to his apprehension. It helped clear out the muddle his thinking had devolved into.

"I *want* to try."

"Then that's all that matters."

A "but" curled through his thoughts. There had to be more, surely. Was it that simple? It felt like it was. The odious burden roosting on his shoulders and pulverizing his heart eased off like a summer storm, here and gone, its booming thunders, black clouds and gloom saved for another day.

"Just to be clear, I don't dislike you. I don't even know you."

That was nice to hear. The first part admittedly more than the last, but the reassurance was kind of her.

"Also, I know how it feels to be seen only when someone needs you." She tightened her lips together, a flintiness catching the dark of her eyes.

"Boyfriend?" he guessed. He didn't expect her to nod curtly.

*"Ex,"* she stressed.

"Out of the picture?" he wondered, but not for himself. He wasn't marking his territory with her or anything. He only hoped that if this guy was bad enough to warrant her cynicism, he wasn't in her life anymore.

She brushed flyaway strands from her face and studiously kept her focus ahead and on Zara. "Yeah, he is."

"Good." Satisfied, he smiled fully, his heart beating faster when she flickered a shy glance at him. It loosened his tongue into returning the favor. She had shared a part of her bravely, and he wished to do the same. "By this time tomorrow, I'll have signed a possibly world-altering deal."

"Is it really that?" She looked as she sounded: unconvinced.

He chuckled. That earned a smile from Maryan. "I'll be working with a Turkish natural gas and oil company to begin drilling in the Indian Ocean off Somalia's coast. With the blessing of the federal government of Somalia."

"It sounds like it'll be a lot of work, but I'm guessing it's good for bringing jobs and stability to people who desperately need it."

"That's what I'm hoping," he said before switching to Somali, "I want to give back to our home."

"It's good of you." Her Somali was soft and unaccented, and achingly comforting to hear.

They lapsed into a natural silence until the steward came up to report from the captain that they would be moving now. Faisal cleared them to leave port and gave instructions for their lunch to be served in the dining room below deck.

Almost alone again, Faisal asked her, "Will you be staying at my home?"

"I booked a hotel in the Fatih district." She gave him the name of the hotel.

A stone's throw from the Eminönü pier. The boutique hotel she picked was a reputably good option in one of Istanbul's ancient quarters. She'd have the luxury of unrivaled historic sights within walking distance and the assurance of a good night's sleep.

"Can I convince you to change your mind?" He asked without giving it much thought. Once he realized what he'd done, there was no taking it back.

Maryan stared at Zara quietly and long enough that he presumed she might not have heard him. Or he might not have even asked after all.

Finally, she regarded him with a slow tilt of her head. "I won't feel comfortable living with you, even temporarily."

He understood that and countered with a solution.

"I have guest quarters outside of my home. I'd be happy to move out temporarily." This way he was convinced he wouldn't feel like a complete troll for forcing more distance between Maryan and Zara. They'd be parting eventually. It was inevitable. He would fight to keep Zara. He needed the nanny to know that. Both his drive to be Zara's father and his commitment to make Maryan's stay in Istanbul—*with him*—as good an experience as it could be.

"I won't be putting you out?" Her wavering commitment to the hotel put wind under the sails of his hope.

"Not one bit, or I wouldn't have suggested it." He presented her a smile to sell the idea on her.

And just to add pressure, he remarked, "Zara will like having you with her, I bet."

She hummed with a sharp look in her eye that hinted she was onto him and his tactics.

Despite that, his efforts worked when she agreed, "Okay. I'll have to call and cancel the reservation."

"I'll reimburse any nonrefundable deposit," he pitched in.

She slung a blithe smile his way. "That won't be necessary," she said before striding over to Zara, leaving him standing awkwardly alone to watch after her for far longer than his sudden feverishly warm body could seem to handle.

And he had invited her to his house. Damn.

# CHAPTER THREE

FAISAL SPENT THE next two hours on his yacht fretting low-key about having Maryan at his home for her two-week stay in Istanbul.

He continued to worry right up to the point that they docked and disembarked onto dry land. They entered the awaiting car and headed toward his home.

In the back seat, Zara was alert and asking questions about where they were headed next. "Are we going on another boat?"

Maryan answered her patiently, hesitant when she said, "No, we're going to your dad's home."

Faisal heard what she left unsaid. That his home was Zara's home as well now.

He wondered if she was still upset with him. They had talked on the yacht. And he'd gotten the profound sense she cared for Zara even more than he initially presumed. He'd also shared more with her in a short time of knowing her than he'd done with any stranger or acquaintance in a long while. Faisal pondered why that was, and then when his temples began to throb, he stopped. No point in driving himself to a headache over why he'd spilled his guts. Or why Maryan hadn't kicked him when he'd been down. All this time he had been telling himself that what the nanny thought didn't matter...

And then she made him feel good.

*Guess that means I do care what the nanny thinks.*

Maryan had been in Zara's life more than he had up until this point. She knew his daughter better than he did. For that reason alone it mattered what she thought. These next two weeks could either go well with her...

*Or go terribly*, he thought with a grim finality.

Faisal couldn't rid himself of the image of Maryan reporting back to Salma and ending any chance he had of keeping Zara. He told himself it was silly. Maryan hadn't shown any signs of deceit when they'd talked on the yacht. Her blunt honesty had calmed his nerves. Someone that frank couldn't plot behind his back.

His driver turned the car onto the private road leading to Faisal's house. They climbed higher up the forested hillside to his home, and he listened as Zara "oohed" and "aahed" from the back of the car.

Her innocent awe brought a smile to his face and lightened the load pressing over his heart.

"Are we there yet?" she asked.

Faisal looked back, his eyes snagging Maryan's gaze before he turned to his daughter. "Almost." He pointed out the window at a break in the trees and their full foliage. "I love looking out at the city from up here."

Zara pressed her small hands to the window and exclaimed, "Look, Maryan! We can see *everything*!" When Maryan didn't move fast enough, she tossed a look back over her shoulder at her nanny. "Are you looking, Maryan? You're going to miss it!"

Caressing Zara's braids lovingly, Maryan hummed. "I'm looking, honey. It's a pretty sight, isn't it?"

Faisal beamed. Pride puffed billowing heat through him. It was worth craning his neck back and straining against his seat belt to experience the moment with them.

The car climbed higher and higher, slowing on the incline's final leg before leveling in front of an impressive set of iron gates. The gates lurched open after Faisal swiped the entry code into his phone. The driver moved the car past the barrier up and around the circular driveway. They stopped before the three-car garage. His mansion sitting ahead of them, in all its shining white stone glory.

"Wow," Zara exclaimed, her seat belt flying off

and her hands gripping the back of his seat. She was close enough that her elation rang shrilly in his ear. "Is that your home, Daddy?"

"Not just my home, Zara. It's your home now, too," he said slowly, carefully.

He caught Maryan's eyes then. She held a guarded expression. None of her stunning features hinted as to her thoughts. He couldn't help but hope he hadn't crossed her by his statement. It was the truth. For now, this was Zara's home. And he wished it would remain that way forever. Maryan's blessing would be the cherry on top, that was all. At least…that was what he convinced himself this was. That he cared what Zara's nanny thought because Maryan was important to his daughter. She was attractive, but that wasn't his driving force.

"Can I get out now?" Zara looked eagerly between them, her eyes practically sparkling when she looked outdoors and spied her new home.

Maryan didn't lift her stare from him. Almost as if she waited on his word for their next action.

Knowing exactly what he'd like to do next, Faisal smiled and said, "Yes, let's start the tour."

The tour of the apartment above his garage ended half an hour later with Zara asking, very sweetly, whether she'd be allowed to watch television in his bedroom.

Faisal had a ninety-eight-inch flat-screen in his room complete with a top-notch home theater system. The walls were soundproof, too, so he could blast his music or Turkish dramas from the comfort of his bed knowing that he didn't have to worry about what lay beyond his spare bedroom.

He knew that wasn't what interested his little girl. She'd seen the large TV screen and goggled at it. When they had stepped out onto the balcony off his bedroom she had momentarily forgotten the television. But now that they'd reentered the room and apartment, she had looked pleadingly up at him to watch her cartoons.

"Sure, why not?" Indulging her, he set her up on the bed and showed her how to control the home theater using the same remote as the television. And when he asked her to show him what he'd taught her, she huffed and rolled her eyes comically.

"Daddy, I know how to do it!"

Trying not to laugh, he said, "Show me anyway."

She humored him and demonstrated perfectly that she did in fact know how to work the remote and the myriad commands installed in it. "See," she scoffed, her ego sounding like it took a hit. "Mommy has three big TVs, too. One for me, one for her and one for anyone who visits."

Of course Salma did. She wasn't a billionaire, but she had plenty of wealth from her modeling and now her acting.

"Okay, sweetheart. Call me or Maryan if you need us." He dropped a kiss atop her head and walked out of the bedroom.

He headed for the kitchen, where he'd left Maryan when she opted out of the tour of his apartment. Wondering again if she disliked him, he strode toward her with less confidence in his swagger as to where he stood with Zara's beautiful nanny. He gulped subtly when she turned away from the electric kettle she was plugging into a wall outlet.

The kitchen island stood between them.

She grasped the sparkling white Calacatta marble countertop. Rich gold veins streaking uniformly through the marble. It had been delivered from Italy as a gift from an Italian investor who owned commercial property in the Calacatta region. What would have cost a hefty purse had cost him nothing, and now Maryan's hands explored the counter's edges nervously.

"I've put on tea," she said softly.

"I'd love a cup of *çay*." Some people preferred coffee; tea was his fuel. He blamed his Somali heritage. His mother and father *loved* their tea. And, of course, tea was a staple in Turkey. It was built into both cultures, Somali and Turkish.

Steeped into their routines, traditions, stories and lives. He was taught to never refuse a cup of tea when offered.

"*Çay?*" she echoed.

"Sorry, that's just 'tea' in Turkish."

She nodded her understanding before drumming her fingernails on the counter, her grasp on it not looking any less nervous.

He didn't like that she was tense around him. And he didn't know why he should care, but he did and wanted it to stop.

"Did you find the tea leaves? Or do you prefer bags?" He had both, mostly for convenience. Sometimes the ritual of preparing tea was pleasant. Other times he was entrenched in a business meeting and popped out for a quick cup of tea. The simpler and faster the better.

She turned to mind the kettle, replying over her shoulder. "I found loose leaves."

"My stash," he said with a grin, blushing when she looked back at him, her hands holding two mugs.

"Stash?"

Face warming a little more, he murmured, "Yeah. I keep tea stocked always, here and in the main house." And as she likely noticed, he stocked a variety, too. His tea preference changed with the weather, the seasons, even his moods. Not every occasion could be black tea—even if his parents preferred traditional black tea as most Somalis often did.

"Were you hiding it? Your stash, I mean," she clarified. "Because I might have had more trouble if you hadn't had everything labeled so very neatly." She lifted the kettle, poured hot water into the two mugs and replaced the kettle on its stand before turning back and finishing with the mugs. "Do you prefer sugar?"

"No, I add honey. I'll grab it," he said, and helped her by fetching a tray and depositing a jar of clover honey on it. He placed the tray on the kitchen island and waited on her to finish with the tea and face him again. What he desired most right then was sitting down with her and finishing their conversation on the yacht. He wanted to know more about her. More about how she'd come into Zara's life when she looked to be in her mid- to late twenties. Young enough to be living out her own life, not tying herself to big responsibilities.

"Seriously speaking, I've never appreciated a kitchen before, but yours is tidy and put-together and very unlike anything I have seen. I can't imagine what the main house looks like."

Maryan's praise triggered a breezy laugh from him. "You'll have to thank Lalam. She's worked her magic here and almost everywhere else in my home."

"Who?" She eyed him funnily, suspicion leaking into her voice.

And he had a guess as to why. She suspected he had a woman in his life. He didn't know whether to be slightly irked by her unvoiced assumption. It wasn't as though he couldn't date and have a woman over for fun. Though that was all it would ever be. Fun. Nothing serious. Romance had never been a serious subject for him. Right then it was the last thing he'd think to do, especially now that Zara had arrived to live full-time with him.

"My housekeeper, three times a week. You'll like Lalam. She speaks enough English, too, so you won't need me to translate."

The aromatic smell of herbal *çay* flooded the kitchen soon after. It lured him from around the kitchen island closer to her with the tray and jar of honey. There was something about her being in his space. The sight of Maryan making herself at home in his kitchen tempted him to disrupt her tea-making process.

She noted his nearness when she glanced up. Unable to hide her startle, she gazed wide-eyed at him for a handful of heart-stopping seconds before looking away shyly.

He read her shyness clear as day and as bright as the afternoon sun shining through the open blinds of the picture windows across the room.

Normally he would've taken that as a sign to charm her. But he wasn't flirting. He shouldn't want to flirt with her, either. Maryan was leaving in fourteen days. She would no longer be Zara's nanny when she boarded her flight home to California. And he wasn't *really* planning to hire her, so...

*I won't sleep with her.*

That would be cruel. To him, to her and probably to Zara most especially. If they did make love, that was all it would be. The intimacy never left his bedroom, not with anyone—not even Zara's mother. They hadn't married as Salma hadn't wanted to, and he didn't believe in love all too much. At least, love felt like it could happen for anyone *but* him.

As if pounding it into his head and tattooing it into his flushed skin and beating heart, he thought, *no kissing and no sex.*

Nothing remotely romantic with Maryan. He wouldn't tease himself with a friendship, either. Though he hoped they could be amicable during her stay. He could pick her brain about Zara. After all, that was all he should be worrying about: whether his daughter would be happy in his care.

Even as he thought that, his mind wandered to Maryan. He studied her.

Aboard his yacht when they got to talking, she displayed a sharp, bright mind, a fierce protective instinct and a keen perception that had him standing taller before her. And not even a boardroom full of his most important stakeholders and external board directors could do that to him.

Maryan managed it in less than the few hours he'd been in her company.

It was a remarkable feat. One she'd never know about, as he would have to reveal the degree to which she affected him.

"It's ready," she said, setting the mugs on the tray.

He lifted it and walked them to the breakfast table across the kitchen and beside the large windows with their sublime views. His garage apartment was one of his favorite spots to relax. Later, he planned to show her his backyard and the treats it held. But now he'd enjoy this cup of tea made by her and ease them into another enlightening conversation.

Last time he had learned about her ex-boyfriend and her aunt and uncle's restaurant. This time he wanted to hear more about her.

*Her and Zara*, he corrected.

Her phone pinged as he opened his mouth to speak.

Maryan mumbled, "Excuse me," and checked her phone. She frowned prettily and tapped a button before setting her phone facedown on the glass table. "Sorry," she said.

"Don't be," he told her, and held out the honey jar after he'd stirred the clover honey into his minty herbal tea. Their fingertips touched when she accepted the jar from him.

He sipped his mug and hummed his approval. "Sage tea. Good choice."

Her phone went off again. Chiming once, twice, three times. He lost count after that and remained quiet, observing her discreetly while imbibing his tea and savoring its honeyed earthy notes while wishing he had a slice of lemon on the side with it. By the umpteenth chime, though, his nosiness got the better of him.

"Your family?" he wondered.

"My friends," she replied with an abashed frown. "I'm sorry. I posted the pictures from earlier."

He pieced the rest together. "Of us, you mean."

"One of all three of us, yes. You, me *and* Zara." It wasn't his faulty hearing; she emphasized Zara's presence in the photo.

Smirking nevertheless, Faisal asked, "Did you tag me in it?"

"No. I didn't want to send the vultures your way." A beat passed, and then she sheepishly added, "They're really nice, actually. *Normally.* Except when they scent drama."

He laughed. Hard. Belly-heaving gusts of laughter. One, because she compared her friends to scavenging birds of prey. And two, because she looked adorably frazzled. It went at odds with the levelheaded persona she had when she confronted him about being late for the airport pickup.

"I'm glad you're having a laugh at my expense," she grumbled, though he caught a thread of humor belying her tone.

"Tag me. I can handle their questions."

"No way," she said quickly. She clutched her phone in both hands now like she worried that he'd take it from her and tag himself in the photo. Calming down, she lowered her hands and muttered, "Trust me. I'm saving you the grief of handling them."

"You're close, then."

She nodded. "Friends from high school and college."

"How much do they know about…?" He fanned a hand between them, the other clutching the handle of his mug.

"About me being here with Zara? Mostly everything…"

He chuckled when she shyly trailed off. Reading between the lines, he made an educated guess as to what she hadn't elucidated for her friends. He could have left it there, but he felt devilish and—despite firmly being convinced he wasn't flirting—he teased, "What don't they know?"

She sipped her tea, commenting, "This *is* good."

"I'm waiting," he joked, seeing through her delay tactics. She wasn't getting away with it.

Sighing, Maryan confessed quietly, "I haven't told them about staying here."

"At my place." He nodded thoughtfully. "But up until a few hours ago, you were booked into a hotel."

"True, but they're asking for pictures of the hotel room."

"Feel free to take photos of your guest room. Or any part of the house, for that matter." He waved in the direction of the main house. He planned a tour of it as well when he showed her to her room, after they'd finished their tea and pulled Zara from the TV.

"That's kind of you, but it doesn't feel right lying to them. I'll just ghost them for now." She shut her phone off and placed it on the table again.

No sooner had she closed her phone did his vibrate. It hummed in his palm as he pulled it from his pocket and regarded the caller ID.

"It's my mom." He rose to his feet. "Do you mind if I take the call?"

She shook her head, excusing him to answer the incoming call from his mother.

He had a feeling he knew why she was calling, but it wasn't until he answered and barely squeezed a "salaam" in before his mom pelted him with questions about Zara.

"Yes," he said as he walked away from Maryan, casting a glance back when he added, "she arrived safely with her nanny."

Faisal stepped into another room. Not the bedroom where Zara was watching her cartoons, the sound of the television spilling out into the hall. He walked into a room that looked like a study. Bright white bookshelves built into the walls and a wide, L-shaped mahogany desk formed the glimpse she saw before he closed the door for privacy to take his call from his mother.

She drank her tea, ruminating on the events that had brought her here. Anything to keep her from wondering what he had to be telling his mom.

A horrifying notion struck her then.

*What if he tells her I'm staying here?*

The mortifying thought stuck with her long enough for her tea and his to grow cold. Deciding to reheat their mugs, she walked them over to an expensive-looking microwave drawer. She figured out how to reheat and set a timer for a minute. Pacing alongside the island table, she found her eyes swiveling back to the door Faisal was behind, her mind racing over the embarrassing thought she'd had. The squalling beep of the microwave startled her.

And if that wasn't enough, Faisal's smooth,

deep voice floating up from behind her added to her jumpiness.

Realizing he'd spooked her, he raised his hands up with palms facing out. "Sorry. I thought you heard me." Then he noticed the spill on the countertop. Noted her clutching her hand. "You scalded yourself."

"Nothing I can't fix." She clenched her teeth for a semblance of a smile and stuck her hand under cold running water briefly.

He fetched her a paper towel, but before that he took her hand, surprising her with his gentle touch and wrinkled brows emanating his worry. Faisal stroked his thumb lightly over the stinging, reddened skin on the back of her hand. Splotchy with angry color from where the hot tea had spilled onto her.

Maryan already hadn't expected his touch.

She wasn't even prepared for when he lowered his head and blew cool air over the heated surface of her sparking flesh. The shiver quaking through her was a force that shut down any rational thought and sharpened her primal senses. She stared at the top of his bowed dark head, his flawless deep brown skin and his slightly parted lips as he concentrated on the task of cooling her hand down.

She could probably let this go on longer.

She knew better, though, and stammered, "It's f-fine. Really. The redness should fade."

"And the pain? How's that?"

She gave it a thought. It stung a bit, but no more than she believed it ought to. "I'm used to working in a restaurant. At worse it's a little burn, at best a night's worth of discomfort."

"So, no first aid kit?"

Maryan gave him a headshake. "But an ice pack would be nice."

"You mean my blowing didn't help?"

She watched the teasing grin overtake his worried look; his handsomeness dialed up to high in the span of a heartbeat.

"It was nice…" She trailed off, and he picked up the ball she dropped.

"It's not an ice pack, though." Chuckling, he released her hand to open the freezer and pull out an ice pack. Wrapping it with the paper towel, he handed it to her.

"I'll grab our tea. Go ahead and sit down."

She heeded his instruction, her chest tight but not in an unpleasant or alarming way. Even if she wanted to argue, it would be hard to do it around the thickness closing off her throat, making breathing harder than it normally should be.

*All because he touched me, blew on my hand, flirted with me?*

He wasn't flirting, though. He'd *joked* with her

and been kind enough to help her ice the burn on her hand. Allowing her brain to spin the moment into a big yarn would be foolish.

*Foolish and a waste of time.*

She had two weeks starting today to settle Zara into her new life with her dad. What she should be doing was getting to know the man who would be taking over her role as caregiver, not weighing every gesture and every look as a gateway into a passionate fantasy starring him and her.

She had to leave her fantasizing at the door until this trip was over.

"It's my fault the tea got cold. My fault you got injured." He joined her at the table with their freshly reheated mugs.

"I was going to reheat mine anyway. It made sense to do the same for you."

"Well, thank you," he said, lifting his mug to his lips and pausing to blow over its surface before a sip.

The memory of his lips hovering over her hand and his cooling breath skating over her sent a fresh shiver through her.

"My mom says hello."

"You told her about me." She wished she didn't sound so squeaky, but her nervousness was amplified at the thought of him telling his mother of their living arrangement.

Reading her mind, he replied, "I left out mention of your staying with me and Zara."

Maryan had trouble masking her relief, because he laughed low and sexily.

"Worried?"

"A little," she admitted blushingly. "I know how Somali parents can be."

Faisal laughed louder this time. "Mine are no different. My mom's especially keen for me to be married."

"Aren't most Somali *hooyo* like that?" It felt natural slipping into their native tongue with him. She'd done it on his flashy boat, and she was doing it now in his equally impressive home. Something about him lowered her normally sky-high thorny defenses.

"You mentioned your aunt and uncle. Your parents?"

"In Hamar—er… Mogadishu." She was used to calling her Somali home city by its local moniker, Hamar.

He grinned wide. "I thought I heard an Hamari accent."

"I must not have gotten rid of it." She'd lived more than half her life in the States. Somalia should be well in her rearview by now. A fond thing she pulled from her memory vault when nostalgia swayed her in that direction, much as she would a childhood toy or book. It wasn't like she ever planned to uproot her life to move back home. And yet it *was* home. Her family lived there. Her mother and father, and brothers and sisters. They made it impossible to fully label her childhood in Somalia as a thing of her past.

"Do you visit?" Faisal asked, taking a bigger gulp of his tea and prompting her to imbibe from her mug.

When her mouth was clear, she said, "I haven't since I moved away. What about you?"

"My family doesn't live in Istanbul. After retiring, my mom and dad left the city for a quieter life in a small town. My younger sister lives with them. I don't get to visit often, but I do try to get away from work for big family occasions. Birthdays, my parents' anniversary, the last days of Ramadan and both Eids."

"Does Zara know her grandparents?" She'd lived with her father and mother in Istanbul for a few years. She must have gotten to know Faisal's side of the family then.

"Oh, yeah. They love her. It's why my mom called. She was pushing for me to bring her soon. We'll likely go after you leave, though."

Of course. That would make sense. It wasn't like he could invite her to go with them. What would his family think?

"But that's not a problem today. Right now

what I'd like to know is what do you want to see most in Istanbul?"

What *did* she want to see in Istanbul?

A myriad of answers came to mind. The Asian side of Istanbul, the city's many mosques, the gilded halls and salons and crystal staircases of Dolmabahçe Palace.

*The famed Hagia Sophia.*

"I'm still technically on the job," she said, dampening the excitement his question unfurled in her.

Salma hadn't stopped paying her. In fact, she'd offered an overly generous severance bonus to Maryan after she agreed to take Zara to her father. The financial incentive hadn't been what motivated her. Being with Zara for a little longer was all the motive she needed to pause her life in California temporarily and hop on a transatlantic flight to Istanbul. But she also wasn't unhappy to see the extra zeros on the bonus check. Especially after what had happened with her ex, Hassan.

Thinking of him annoyed her. Knowing that she'd wasted three and a half years on him boiled her blood. All of that didn't compare to what he had done to her *and* her aunt and uncle at the end.

It was one thing to be angry at her, but her Aunt Nafisa and Uncle Abdi had done nothing to deserve being robbed. And by their sous-chef of all people.

*The jerk.*

She stewed in her chair and looked away from Faisal, afraid he'd see her anger and ask questions. She wouldn't be able to handle any of them with grace. Talking about her thieving ex-boyfriend infuriated her. She'd told Faisal enough already about the subject. Saying any more would be assuming that he was interested in hearing her rant.

"Okay, but I'm not tethering you to the house," he said with a frown. "You're free to go where you want. Take Zara with you. I'd like her to see Istanbul."

"And where will you be?" She ignored the alarm bell clanging in her head and the tightening mix of panic and ire pressing down onto her thumping heart. Leaping to a conclusion wouldn't do her any good.

"As I said, I'll be busy closing this partnership deal for my company. But by tomorrow afternoon, my schedule is free." His face relaxed, his frown softer and his eyes less troubled. The dark beginnings of a beard raked his jaw and climbed to his high-boned cheeks. He palmed the lower half of his face, his nostrils twitching with an audible sigh.

Suddenly the air around him shifted.

He smiled charmingly. "I was thinking a city tour might be a good way to celebrate the closing of this deal. If that's something you'd be interested in? I'm a pretty good tour guide."

His smile unleashed a fluttering in her stomach and a rush of heady warmth over her body.

"I think Zara would like that," she said.

"And you?"

She heard the rest of his question. *Would* you *like it?*

After drinking down to the dregs in her cup, Maryan placed it on the tray and watched as Faisal mirrored her with his mug. She stood and grabbed the tray handles, her eye contact with him unsevered and stronger than before. He tensed his shoulders slightly as if anticipating her rejection. Even so, his smile remained sunny on his too-handsome face.

"I've always wanted to see the Hagia Sophia."

It took a few seconds, but his bright teeth flashed at her. "Then we'll add it to the tour." He stared at her afterward, his smile edging on playful and his eyes dropping to her mouth.

"Sounds good," she agreed.

"It's a date," he added.

She couldn't unglue her tongue from the roof of her mouth to give him a comeback. So she did the next best thing. Bobbed her head, lifted the tray with their empty mugs and walked away from him before she combusted from blushing too much.

# CHAPTER FOUR

MARYAN ANTICIPATED ONLY one thing from her second day in Turkey. It wasn't her usual morning routine of stretching, doing yoga poses and squeezing in a shower. It wasn't even her break from that routine when she spent half an hour longer than usual on her makeup.

It was Faisal taking her and Zara out to tour the city.

She lowered her makeup brush from the apple of her cheeks, the creamy blush adding a glow to her face and her contouring more perfect than usual. Even her experimentation with eyeshadow colors turned out beautifully. She'd worn less makeup having taken into account that they'd be walking and touring Istanbul. A summerlike breeze wafted into her grand guest room from the open balcony doors and had her appreciating her choice of adding sunscreen beneath her sheer tinted moisturizer. After their tea, Faisal had showed her to her room in the main house. If she had thought his apartment was luxurious, the main house was near palatial, her room being no exception.

She stared at the woman gazing back at her in the reflection of the wide, beautifully framed dresser mirror. Maryan barely recognized herself, but in the best way possible.

Liking what she saw, she uncapped her setting spray and closed her eyes. She spritzed around her face twice and opened her eyes when the satiny mist rested coolly over her skin.

Refreshed from her morning routine, she stood to close the balcony doors. Instead of stopping, though, she ventured outdoors, the sun-warmed stone of the balcony heating the soles of her bare feet. She stopped before the balustrade to be awed by the vista once again. She'd done it plenty of times since Faisal showed her to the room.

"Breathtaking," she whispered, her lips drawing up into a smile.

Her thoughts meandered from verdant treetops, the swooping valley and the panoramic city scene bisected by the shimmering strip of the Bosporus as the sun crept higher over the horizon. She wondered what her aunt and uncle could be up to right then. It was late for her family and friends in California. Nearly midnight. But she knew that was when Aunt Nafisa and Uncle Abdi sat in the living room winding down from another long day at their restaurant. They were late sleepers yet early risers for as long as she'd been living with them.

*Fifteen years this fall.*

Fifteen years since she'd left her parents and younger siblings and flew from the only home she'd once known in Mogadishu to live with her maternal aunt and her husband. Now Aunt Nafisa and Uncle Abdi were the only family she cared to recognize.

Scowling at the thought of her mom and dad, Maryan breathed deeply and pushed down the flush of anger threatening to rise. She'd been holding on to it for so long that bottling her resentment had grown to be a natural instinct.

They hadn't asked if she wanted to leave for a life in America. In their eyes, feeding seven children had become too much. They could convince themselves they'd given her a better chance to live, but the truth was her parents had been poor and desperate enough to push one of their children from the nest. As the eldest, she was the unlucky child.

*But then I wouldn't have met Aunt Nafisa and Uncle Abdi.*

Her aunt and uncle were the one bright spot in all this. Bright enough to blast the frosty anger that tended to grip her whenever she deigned to think of her parents. And she knew it wasn't their fault they were poor, but...

*If they had asked, it wouldn't be like this.*

She wouldn't feel something suspiciously close to *hate* every time she thought of how they'd made a life-altering decision for her.

She'd been twelve. Plenty old enough to make a choice for herself.

*Or at least feel like they included my feelings in their decision-making.*

Maryan blew out the breath she'd been holding reflexively.

Forcing her thinking away from her parents, she remembered what Faisal had told her yesterday on his sailing yacht about his plan for striking oil in Somalia. His earnest expression and voice came flooding to mind.

*I want to give back to our home,* he'd said.

It was an impassioned statement and a bold one at that. For his sake she prayed it worked out. There were plenty of families in Somalia—poor ones like hers who could use a change in fortune like Faisal's promising business plan. A boom in oil would lift up the whole nation and might even put it more firmly toward a direction of steadier and more rapid economic development and progress.

If she saw anyone being capable of doing it, it was Faisal Umar. Billionaire. Successful tycoon.

*Single dad.*

That should have stopped her fantasizing about Zara's handsome father.

But thinking of him made her wonder what he had planned for their city tour. It wasn't her imagination that made her heart thump a little faster and a jitteriness swarm her empty stomach. She would've chalked it up to needing breakfast, except she wasn't thinking about food.

She was still fixated on Faisal.

And if she wasn't careful, she'd forget why she had come to Istanbul in the first place.

*Zara is why I'm here.*

All thoughts of Faisal and his unwarranted effect on her vanished when she turned her head sharply from the view out on her balcony. Someone was knocking on the guest room door. It couldn't be Zara. She had checked in on her ten minutes earlier and she'd been sound asleep in the room next door.

Believing it to be Faisal, she crossed into the room and answered the door.

The tall, fair-haired young woman on the other side wasn't him.

Her rosy-cheeked smile invited Maryan into asking, "Are you Lalam?"

"I am, Miss Maryan," Faisal's highly praised housekeeper said, her glowing, lightly freckled face adding to her youthful appearance. She held a serving tray and explained in lovely, lilting English, "I bring you breakfast. I hope it's okay?"

"It's more than okay, thank you, and it's just Maryan." She reached for the tray, but the housekeeper pulled away.

"I carry." Once she was inside the room she veered for the bed. "Is here okay?"

*"Evet."*

Lalam turned to her, her sunny smile growing larger. "You learn Turkish?"

Maryan blushed. She'd been practicing. Since Faisal planned to give her and Zara a tour of the city, she had wanted to immerse herself in the language and experience both. The newly installed Turkish-learning app on her phone was helping. "A little," she told the housekeeper, cringing. "Is it bad?"

Looking to be on the younger side of her twenties, Lalam placed the breakfast tray on the folded duvet cover and spun to her. She hoped it wasn't to tell her to quit practicing Turkish because hers was awful.

"Your Turkish is *çok iyi*. In English: 'very good.'"

Maryan laughed. "Yes, I learned that one early." Faisal predicted she would like Lalam, and she'd have to let him know he was right.

"You like Istanbul?" Lalam gestured to the

open balcony doors and what they could see of the metropolis from Faisal's home.

"I haven't seen too much, but from what I have it's a lovely city. Busy like most cities are, but lots of history to it."

"Very busy city, yes. I move to Istanbul for school. Now I live and study here all the time."

Her English wasn't hard to understand. Maryan was relieved she spoke it at all. Her Turkish wasn't going to magically improve by leaps and bounds in the span of two weeks. And she had a feeling talking to Lalam would give her breaks for some real adult conversation. Something she had a sense she wouldn't get from Faisal too much. Even though he had promised his schedule would be clear this afternoon.

Thinking of him prompted her to wonder, "Is Faisal still sleeping in his..."

She trailed off when Lalam furrowed her brow. Realizing it was possible the housekeeper wasn't aware her boss had spent the night in the swanky garage apartment, she phrased it differently.

"Is he out?"

Lalam clasped her hands in front of her spotless white apron. Her black T-shirt and black jeans must have been part of a uniform. The ensemble did make her look more efficient than Maryan already suspected she was, simply from observing how pleasingly tidy the house was.

All of that was forgotten when Lalam reported, "Mr. Umar is at work, yes."

"Work?" Maryan parroted.

The housekeeper pointed to the breakfast tray. "Mr. Umar leave a message for you."

She noted a small folded paper tucked under the covered plate. The note was in a loopier scrawl than she envisioned Faisal was capable of. The men she'd come across and the ones in her life tended to write blocky and hard print. Like they had a point to prove.

*I promise I'll be back in time.*

For their tour, he meant.

"When did he leave?" She looked up at Lalam, catching the housekeeper walking for the bedroom door.

She turned back. "Very early. I start work. He leave for work. We have little time to say salaam."

Staring down at the message, Maryan barely noted Lalam's departure until she looked up a little while later and found herself alone in the room. The door was closed again like nothing had transpired.

The privacy was welcome, though. She gazed down at his message again, her heart pounding and her anticipation to see him after he finished with his work walking a tightrope. It was enough to ignore the nagging doubt that she should be worrying more about his commitments and his ability to juggle his business *and* his fatherly duties to Zara.

He was running late to meet Maryan and Zara again.

Faisal sped up his walk and jogged the final paces to one of the entrances of the Grand Bazaar. Burak was exactly where he said he'd be waiting. His head of security greeted him with one of his stoic nods, his face devoid of any telling emotions. It was perfect for the job, but this wasn't a job. Faisal had asked him to kick off the city tour in his absence.

*That was two hours ago.*

And now he was late and preparing to grovel and give the best excuse to Maryan.

"Tell me honestly: How bad is it?" If he went in armed with the knowledge, he might be able to reverse the damage he'd done to Maryan's impression of him.

Burak crossed his arms and grunted.

"That bad?" He sighed, knowing he had only himself to blame. After promising Maryan he'd have his schedule free earlier in the day, and not explaining why he had ended up working longer, he expected nothing short of a frosty reception from her. Especially considering she hadn't shied from sharing her opinions before.

He anticipated being chewed out by her. And he was stalling because of it.

"Was she that angry?" he asked in Turkish.

"She hides it well like most women, but it's there. The quiet ones are the scariest. You'll see what I mean soon enough." Burak flung him a wry smile and switched to English, "I don't envy you, boss."

Faisal laughed, a hollow sound.

"I'd warn you to keep your distance, but she knows you're here. I told her when you left the office."

"Yeah, maybe I'd take your advice," Faisal drawled, "but keeping my distance is what got me into this mess." To be specific, the time apart from his daughter. He had no doubt Maryan would hold it over his head like the sword of Damocles.

He hoped she wasn't closed off to his legitimate excuse for being late.

Burak walked him into the bazaar before he stopped and said, "Good luck, boss."

"I'll need it," Faisal rejoined with a sigh.

He pushed forward alone. His gait purposefully slowed as he neared the small covered shop that Burak had pointed out. The shop Maryan and Zara were inside. Beautiful handmade jewelry and wood-carved trinket boxes lined the shelves. The shopkeeper was a young woman wearing a hijab. She greeted him from afar where she helped Maryan behind the glass counter.

Zara saw him first.

"Daddy!"

He opened his arms to catch her embrace and ground them before Zara's exuberance toppled them back into a display stand of cheaper-looking necklaces and bracelets. The more authentic gems and jewelry were guarded under lock and key behind protective glass cases.

Standing, Faisal grasped Zara's hand and listened to her cheery rehashing of how her day with her beloved nanny had panned out thus far. He walked her back to Maryan to face the music. And seeming to understand exactly what he planned, Maryan swung her attention back to the shopkeeper.

"Can I have a look at that mother-of-pearl bracelet?" She touched her finger to the top of the glass counter at her bracelet of choice.

As soon as the shopkeeper was preoccupied with the task, Faisal seized the window to squeeze in the first of what he anticipated would be many apologies today.

"I'm sorry I didn't call or text earlier. I was in a meeting—"

"I get it. You were busy," she interjected in Somali, sounding far from understanding. With a breezy shrug, and still avoiding eye contact, she said, "Zara and I were doing just fine here."

The "without you" hung in the electrified air between them. She needn't have spelled it out for him. She was just as piqued with him as he expected. Burak had given him a fair warning, too.

But it didn't prepare his body for the abject disappointment hardening her voice when she snapped, "You didn't have to rush over on our account. Don't let us stop you from working."

Her words struck his heart.

With a smile that rang fake to him, she then accepted the bracelet from the shopkeeper and switched to English again to thank her.

Realizing that he wouldn't get anywhere with her in their current setting, Faisal held back from saying any more. He allowed Zara to lure him to a part of the store away from Maryan. Their backs turned to her, Zara pointed out a series of beautifully rendered necklaces, anklets, brooches, bracelets, earrings and even cuff links. Gold, silver and copper metal formed the bases, and alluring precious and semiprecious gemstones were inlaid in the metallic frames.

"I like that one," Zara said, smiling toothily up at him.

"This one?" He tapped the glass showcase at the stunning amber necklace. Inlaid into a simple rose-gold case, the polished honey-colored amber was the size of his thumbnail. The threads of pink gold holding the amber pendant looked too fragile for a seven-year-old. But this was a momentous experience. He had Zara living with him now. She was his daughter, and he could do everything he ever dreamed of doing with her since he had stepped in Salma's delivery room and gotten his first peek at Zara inside her bassinet.

"Do you like it that much?" he asked her.

She nodded enthusiastically. "It's so pretty, Daddy!"

He glanced over his shoulder and caught Maryan's darting gaze. She'd been looking at him. Possibly glaring holes into the back of his head from her warranted annoyance.

"Excuse me," he called to the shopkeeper in Turkish. "Can you wrap this one up for me?"

Maryan stubbornly cast her eyes everywhere but at him as he approached her once more. This time to do business with the shopkeeper. Zara bounced up and down in place while she watched her necklace be lovingly packed into a jewelry box and inside a shopping bag. The shopkeeper held it out to her from across the counter, and as soon as she had it she showed Maryan.

Her nanny indulged her with a warmer, genuine smile. Something she hadn't been able to muster for him when he entered the store.

The sterling silver chain bracelet with its iridescent mother-of-pearl stones was on the glass counter where Maryan left it to shower Zara and her new necklace with attention and affection. Deftly he plucked it up by its thin chain and held it out to the shopkeeper.

"Add this too, please." He spoke Turkish, knowing full well Maryan and Zara wouldn't be able to understand.

The shopkeeper did as he requested and quickly packed the bracelet up without alerting Maryan. She smiled knowingly when he tapped his card to pay her for the service. All of this happened in the time that Maryan was looking away.

When she turned, she confronted a second small shopping bag identical to Zara's on the counter over the exact spot that she'd left the bracelet.

She looked at him instantly, her lips parting, her eyes holding a question...*and* an argument to return the purchase.

He made a silent show of tucking his designer wallet inside his suit jacket. The bracelet was paid for. It was hers. A small bracelet was nothing to his immense wealth. And that wealth meant not a thing if it couldn't be enjoyed with others. Co-workers, friends, family.

Maryan was none of those to him. And yet she'd helped raise Zara. He owed her more than a pretty trinket.

"Can we talk?" he asked in Somali.

She briskly nodded and turned to answer Zara's reaching hands and clamoring cry to see the second shopping bag.

"I want to see your present, Maryan!" She bounced for a look but stopped when Maryan handed her the bag. They lingered in the shop until Zara talked her nanny into wearing the bracelet. Then Maryan helped Zara with her necklace. Both of them walked out of the shop wearing smiles and their new accessories.

Faisal had to capture the moment. "Wait. Can I take a picture?"

Maryan was shaking her head when Zara exclaimed, "Yes, please!"

Zara posed with Maryan, who allowed him to take their pictures.

Once he was satisfied, he slipped his phone in his pants pocket and waved Burak over to them.

"Take Zara to the restaurant," he said to his friend and security head.

Zara began protesting, but he crouched down to her level and squeezed her hands. "I need to talk to Maryan quickly."

Maryan helped by stepping up and stroking Zara's braids. "We're right behind you."

"Promise?" Zara asked them, her bottom lip not trembling as noticeably.

"Promise," he said with Maryan. They traded

a quick look before Burak accepted Zara's outstretched hand and led her away from them.

"If this is about you being late *again*…" she began.

"It is, but let's talk elsewhere." He guided her through the populated centuries-old bazaar, down winding alleys, past ancient crumbling sections of walls and under the canopy of arched ceilings decorated with blue mosaic tiles. They emerged out of one of twenty-one entrances into the Grand Bazaar.

Breathing the fresh air outdoors was always a treat. Especially when the breeze was tinged with aromatic flavors of spices, herbs, meats and tea.

"Would you like a cup? It won't spoil our appetite."

With their tea in hand, they found a bench in the square across from the bazaar. Nowhere near as crowded, it was the perfect place to talk to her, and he hoped to plead his case of tardiness. He didn't know which would be more challenging to do: to lay bare his heart or give her the rundown of how he'd failed to secure his coveted partnership deal for Umar Capital Group.

"Where did your security guy take Zara exactly?"

Faisal's heart-stopping grin put her at ease as much as it set up her guard.

"Ever heard of the internet-famous Salt Bae?" He mimed sprinkling salt and laughed breezily. "He's got a restaurant inside the bazaar and it's very popular. And since he's somewhat of a national treasure and this is a tour of Istanbul..."

The mention of the tour reminded her why they were outside and away from Zara.

Trusting his judgment that his daughter was safe in the care of the tall, muscled bodyguard Burak, Maryan focused on delving into what she expected was his apology.

*Might as well get this over with.*

If it was going to be a half-cocked attempt at an apology, she wanted it done and over with, and preferably before her refreshing pomegranate iced tea grew too warm.

"I'm sorry about being late. I am." He sighed and unbuttoned his suit jacket. Shifting on the bench to face her more, he launched into an explanation. "Something came up last-minute at the office. I couldn't leave it to anyone else. All my staff were expecting me to be there. I... It didn't feel right to abandon them."

Without thinking it through, she blurted, "But abandoning your daughter was okay?"

He pulled his handsome features into a grimace. He had to have known he walked *right* into that one. It stung, she bet, but it couldn't be hurting any more than her bruised ego. She'd really believed him—*trusted* in him to come through for her and spend the day with Zara. This wasn't about the tour, she'd told herself, but about whether he could be there for his daughter the way she deserved.

For four years she'd been a rock to Zara. She'd nurtured her confidence and protected her whenever possible.

And now she was passing that long-held torch to Faisal.

*But he's failing.*

He was also doing a terrible job at trying to meet her tall expectations. Even the short ones, like arriving on time, were eluding him right now. If he was going to apologize, would he be passing the blame on to some ambiguous work-related problem that had cropped up conveniently at the last minute?

"The deal's been postponed." Faisal looked down into his paper cup, both hands holding his tea. His face crumpled as he said, "After everyone's effort and hard work, it all managed to fall apart anyway."

She only learned of this deal yesterday, but he'd made it sound important to his company.

*And to him.*

She felt bad for him. Sympathy held her irritation at bay.

"It was going so well, too. The two brothers

who own majority holding of this Turkish natural gas and oil company were happy with the partnership my company would offer."

"They must have explained why," she said.

Faisal barely sipped his cup. He touched the rim to his lips and pulled back to answer her, embarrassment coloring his tone. "They did."

She didn't rush him to elucidate. Looking miserable, he glanced at the passersby in the square. Whatever it was that put the brakes on his hard-sought business deal must have been bad. Especially when it was obvious he was working up the courage to rehash the humiliating explanation.

"I'll show you what went wrong," he finally said, his phone in hand. He pulled up his email and opened attached photos.

"These are recent photos from a magazine. A popular gossip rag published all through Europe. They'd sneaked a paparazzo into the party." He turned his phone for her to have a look at the photos attached to the email. Each photo had him in a compromising position with a different woman. The last one had him pressed between *two* waifish brunettes in skimpy bathing suits.

"Where were you when this was taken?"

"A pool party I attended last week." He tucked his phone away.

She'd read about him being a playboy. It

shouldn't have surprised her that he would be partying the week before his daughter arrived to live with him forever.

Stuffing down her misplaced annoyance, and the more frustrating twinges of jealousy at seeing the photos of him embracing other women, she asked the next most logical question. "Why do they care what you do in your spare time?"

It shouldn't have been anyone's business. Certainly not hers to judge what he did to unwind after a long day's work.

"The host was one of the Turkish brothers. Erkin is his name, and he loves partying. More than me, evidently." His self-deprecating smile plucked her heartstrings. "I know what they call me. A playboy."

She didn't confess to having believed the epithet.

"It's okay," he murmured, his piercing gaze frozen on her. "It's true. I like partying. I work hard, play harder sometimes. Not always. When it's deserved."

"You didn't answer me. Why should you have to explain what you do in your free time?" She wasn't lauding his playboy reputation. She just didn't feel he should be penalized for it. And he wouldn't suffer alone. There were people he might be able to help in Somalia with his oil and natural gas project. Families and communities who would benefit from a healthy economy. Families like hers.

"That was my mistake. I didn't think it'd be polite to refuse the younger brother's invitation. But it seems his older brother is more traditional than I was led to believe. They don't want their company image tarnished by photos like the ones I showed you."

"So, is there hope left to save the deal?"

He heaved a sigh. "There might be, but I'll have to win back the older brother's trust. Prove that I'm not just partying all day and debauching my company's reputation."

"Is that all you wanted to say to me?" Maryan sensed there was more he hadn't let her in on.

Sighing again, he said, "Besides begging you to understand that I normally don't break promises?"

"Yes."

"I don't want you to think I can't work all of this out. Fatherhood and running my business. I'm capable of doing both and not drowning."

His vehement statement was impressive.

It also wasn't enough.

She needed to *see* him putting in the same effort she had no doubt he'd shown to secure his gainful business.

Faisal turned into her a little more, the heat coming off him closer.

"My parents moved from a small town outside of Mogadishu to Turkey thirty years ago. They were business owners in Istanbul. We lived next door to our small family bakery. On weekends, my sister and I would help them by doing whatever we could.

"I watched them juggle us and their business, and they juggled successfully."

"And that's why you believe it'll work for you." She hugged a bare arm around her stomach and narrowed her eyes. Everything he said about his family was a step in the positive direction.

*But it's still not enough.*

"I have to believe it will." He gazed at her with an intensity that made her heart pang.

Softly, she said, "On your boat you said you wanted to try, and I believe you. But you have to *actually* try to be here with Zara."

"I will," he vowed.

"I'm not going to dictate your schedule to you." She wasn't here to tell him how to spend his time. "All I'm asking is that you find more time for Zara."

"I swear I will," he repeated, a smile relaxing his face and making him painfully handsome.

She gulped a bigger sip of her tea than planned and coughed.

He leaned in, his hand falling on her shoulder, his fingers pressing gently. "Are you okay?"

She had cool tangy sweet tea shoot up her nose, but it might be worth the spine-electrifying contact with him. Maryan felt a telltale blush, her dark brown skin warming to the touch and her cheeks aching in her battle to stop from smiling goofily.

"Fine," she murmured. "But we should head back to Zara."

Faisal stood and offered her a hand to help her up from the bench. As they walked back together, he shattered the silence.

"I also hope you'll let me give you that tour of Istanbul while you're here with us?"

He framed it as a question, giving her a chance to refuse. It was a brownie point for him.

"We've seen the bazaar," she said, barely recognizing the good-natured taunt in there. Who was she? Faisal's flirty nature was rubbing off on her obviously.

He laughed and smiled. "I know you don't mean *all* of the bazaar."

"Some of it," she teased.

He guided her past the metal detectors at the bazaar's entrance and drew close enough to bump arms with her and rattle the silver mother-of-pearl bracelet on her wrist. The bracelet he'd gifted to her.

She turned her head and discovered his face inches from hers. Naturally a kiss wasn't far from her mind.

He closed the gap to her ear in a heartbeat and whispered, "Then allow me to show you more."

# CHAPTER FIVE

A FEW DAYS AGO, Maryan hadn't believed Faisal's promise to change all too much. She had learned through life experiences not to trust twice. First with her parents promising they'd see her soon before sending her off to live in America on her own, and then when her thieving ex-boyfriend, Hassan, robbed her and her family.

She hadn't placed stock in his vow to be more present and spend time with Zara.

If she'd been a betting person, she would've lost a lot of money by now. Because Faisal surprised her. Not only had he shown up regularly and on time for their outings the past three days, but he'd shown them plenty of Istanbul. Never taking them to the same place twice. Always showing them a new and beautiful side to the metropolis he called home.

And Maryan had already known this, but Istanbul wasn't merely a concrete jungle. Pockets of green spaces were to be found all over the city. Çamlıca Hill was one of those places.

"Let's go on a picnic," Faisal had said that morning.

Zara had been more than happy with the idea.

After Maryan had wondered whether they'd be distracting him from work, Faisal had assured her that everything that needed his personal attention was seen to before he'd asked them on the impromptu picnic. His exact words echoed in her mind.

*I'd rather spend the day outside with you and Zara than be cooped up in my office.*

It sounded like he was turning a new leaf.

*I don't even know him.*

Certainly not well enough to know whether he had changed or not over these five days. And if the change was truly for the better or otherwise. But he hadn't been late again. And he had managed to keep any promises he made to Zara. It didn't matter what she thought outside of that.

Zara was happy, and that was enough to quiet her doubts about him.

"Maryan, look," Zara whispered in her ear and wrapped her arms around her neck. She surprised her by coming up from behind.

Maryan had been sitting by Faisal while Zara wandered off to explore nearby. She was enamored by the pretty rows of flower gardens lining the footpath. The path wended through the hilltop park. Zara hadn't been alone in exploring it, either. Plenty of children loitered near the flowers, their parents and families sheltered under the umbrage of the trees scattered through the park.

They were under one of those trees now. Sunlight pierced weakly past the net of the wild maple's thick foliage. Even with the shade protecting them from the midafternoon sun Maryan hadn't taken any chances. She'd packed suntan lotion to protect them all. The last thing she wanted ruining their perfect day was a sunburn.

"Daddy's sleeping," she said in Maryan's ear with a giggle.

Maryan looked to her right to find that Zara's reporting was true. Faisal *had* fallen asleep.

They had been chatting about the city, and she'd gotten the sense that he loved Istanbul. But then they'd lapsed into a peaceful silence. She had looked away for what had felt like a handful of minutes, so it was surprising to see him sound asleep.

He was lying on his back on the grass, his arms tucked under his head and his T-shirt stretched tight against his sculpted chest. He was nothing but lean, clean-lined muscle under his finely tailored business suits. She'd discovered over the course of the day that it was more challenging to look away from his hotness when he was wearing a casual T-shirt and denim "manpris" than it was when he was in his work wear.

She raised her eyes up from his body to his gorgeous face. The man could've been a model or actor and given Salma a run for her money. Though now, Maryan understood how they'd been an item once. Two breathtakingly beautiful people gravitating to each other was a tale as old as time.

That wasn't jealousy souring her tongue. Rather the bitter dregs of the spices from the freshly made Turkish tea Lalam had packed for them in a thermos.

It was pointless to be envious when Faisal would never see her like that.

*I wouldn't want him to, anyway.*

Nothing would come from a relationship right now. And one-night stands had never been her thing. Her friends had *urged* her to have meaningless rebound fun after she and Hassan broke up. She wasn't up to it. Even knowing that it would feel good to hurt Hassan. He'd been a cocky jerk. Once she'd believed his charismatic personality was the most attractive part of him. That was before she had realized how toxic his overconfidence could be to her.

Looking at Faisal, she couldn't help but compare his charming persona with her ex's.

*That isn't fair. He isn't Hassan.*

But it didn't change the fact that it would spell trouble for her to mingle with someone equally as magnetic as her ex-boyfriend. The thought alone soured her mouth. It made it all too clear to her that she wasn't ready for romance yet. She wasn't in the headspace to tangle hearts with anyone. Even someone as attractive and good-natured as Faisal.

"Do I wake him up?" Zara moved her arms off Maryan and sat carefully by her dad.

"No, we'll let him sleep." Maryan pressed a finger to her lips and watched as Zara mimed her. She shared a smile with her before glancing at Faisal's relaxed facial features. And because she couldn't stare at him forever, she forced her attention to her phone.

She hadn't answered any of her friends' messages with any details about her trip yet. Any replies to their questions had been vague. But she knew that couldn't last forever. She'd posted more photos to her social feed, and they had gotten plenty of hits. Hundreds of hearts and comments from friends, family and even random people who had followed her over the course of the last few days.

The hashtags she'd been using were new to her but popular in travelers' circles: *#istanbul, #travelbug, #travelgram, #travelwithme*.

One of her favorite photos had the most buzz. It was a photo of her and Faisal atop Galata Tower. They went to the popular tourist spot yesterday. The line into the tower at sundown snaked so long she hadn't thought they'd ever make it to the top. Though after waiting half an hour—and following Faisal's teasing suggestion of using his company's helicopter to see both Galata Bridge and Tower from above—they were admitted inside.

Maryan tapped the photo for a closer look... again. She'd looked at it enough when she had been alone last night.

Faisal kept his arms at his sides, but his posture was relaxed. He leaned on the stone railing at the top of the tower and pulled into her right before Zara snapped the photo. She couldn't help noting they looked *cozy*. And she wasn't alone in thinking so. All she had to do was scroll down to see her friends echoing the same thought.

It seemed *everyone* in her life wanted to know whether Faisal was her rebound after Hassan.

Her aunt and uncle weren't hooked on social media as most people were these days. A blessing in this instance, as they still hadn't caught wind of the online speculation of her love life. And the *only* reason she was 100 percent certain of that was that they'd have texted or called about it by now.

She'd have to burst everyone's bubbles eventually. Crush her friends from hoping that there was anything happening between her and Faisal.

*Nothing has and nothing ever will.*

She posted a new picture. A photo of the snaking garden footpath on Çamlıca Hill. Adding the appropriate tags, she tapped to post. No sooner had she when her notification bell alerted her to new activity. Maryan sighed. Apparently even a safe, Faisal-free photo like the one she posted warranted curiosity from friends.

*Maybe I should clear the air and tag him.*

Faisal had suggested it on the first day. Now it wasn't looking like a bad idea.

Before Maryan could give it any more thought, Zara pulled her out of her thinking with a question.

"When you leave, will it just be Daddy and me?"

Her heart thumping a little faster, Maryan hummed softly, tucked her phone away, and scooted closer to where Zara sat by her father. She squeezed both of Zara's small shoulders before pulling her back into her open arms. Zara fell gently and willingly into the comforting embrace.

With Zara's head tucked under her chin, Maryan sought to calm any doubt in the young girl.

"Unfortunately, I can't stay forever." In fact, she was due to leave in a little more than a week. She gulped at the reality. Somehow her time in Istanbul was coming to a speedier close than she'd hoped it would.

When she spoke next it seemed as though she were convincing herself of her encroaching departure as much as Zara. "It's going to take some getting used to. But I hope you try for your dad's sake."

"Will you miss me?"

Maryan rocked her side to side, her voice a hoarse but emphatic whisper when she answered, "Yes. Of course I will."

"Do you think Nadia and Simone miss me?"

Nadia and Simone were her school friends. The trio were inseparable. Maryan had spent countless days planning playdates for Zara and her friends, minding the children when the other girls' parents couldn't spare time away from their jobs.

"I'm sure they do. But you have their numbers. You can call them on your phone." She hadn't approved of Salma giving Zara a phone, but now it would come in handy. "And you can always call me, too."

In the smallest voice, Zara glumly stated, "That's not true. I tried calling them today, and they didn't answer me."

"When did you call?"

"Don't be angry." Zara turned in her arms, her bottom lip protruding and her wide brown eyes begging Maryan's forgiveness. "I stayed up last night to call them."

"Oh, honey," Maryan began, tamping down the instinct to scold her. Sleep was important, but Zara was clearly hurt that her friends hadn't answered her call even when she'd phoned them at an appropriate time. Maryan had explained the eleven-hour time difference from Istanbul to Los Angeles, and Zara had been listening well. Still, despite her effort, she was disappointed by her friends.

"Why didn't they answer, Maryan?"

She chose to ignore that Zara had stayed up past her bedtime. There was a time and place to chastise her behavior later. Now wasn't it.

"I don't know, sweetheart." She stroked Zara's cheek and smiled to soften the blow. "Sometimes people can disappoint us."

Zara sniffed and burrowed her face into Maryan's shirt. Her quiet sobs shuddered through her small body. The anvil pressing down onto Maryan's chest crushed her heart as she held Zara through her tearful display.

It wasn't fair that she should be feeling this way.

Worse, it felt so familiar to her. She wasn't much older than Zara when she'd been sent away to live in America. The confusion of assimilating into a new culture, of making new friends and adapting to a whole new life apart from everything and everyone she'd known in Somalia, had been the toughest part.

*No*, she corrected sharply. Because eventually she *did* adapt. With the help and support of her aunt and uncle, Maryan had survived. What she hadn't recovered from was the painful knowledge that her parents could live without her.

She couldn't quiet the idea that they'd used her.

Like Hassan had used her for a job and then after their breakup didn't have the shred of decency to walk away but robbed her and her family instead.

Now here was Zara feeling lonely and adrift. And she was leaving her, too, so it wasn't like she had a leg to stand on. But she'd meant it about never forgetting her. Trouble was, Maryan wasn't certain her promise made any impact.

Absorbed with comforting Zara, she forgot about Faisal.

It was an upsetting surprise then when he sat up suddenly.

"What's the matter?" He phrased it like a question, but with his steely eyes and gruff tone, it was unmistakably a demand. She couldn't blame him for it, either. What parent wouldn't be annoyed to wake up to find their child distraught in the arms of their nanny?

Zara saved her from a response.

She pulled out of Maryan's arms and turned to her dad, sniffling loudly before clutching him like she had Maryan.

He hugged her tightly. As though his arms were shield enough from her big worries.

"I'll stretch my legs," Maryan said, a yearning flourishing in her. For what, she couldn't name.

At least she couldn't until Faisal gave her the tersest of nods.

Dismissed, she rose to her feet, an epiphany dawning on her. She'd wanted him to stop her. The farther she walked from them, the more she longed for him to call her back, to ask her to stay while he took over assuaging Zara's fears. Fears he might not fully understand or appreciate. She had the unique perspective of being dumped in America by her parents. It wasn't so far off from Zara's situation. Cultural shock, a loss of friends, a sense of displacement—she'd experienced all of that.

*Faisal doesn't know that, though.*

Because surely if he had he wouldn't have accepted her leaving…

*Would he?*

Faisal began doubting whether it had been a wise choice to let Maryan leave. It was difficult to ask her to stay when he recalled their conversation from a few days back outside the Grand Bazaar.

She'd said she believed he could be there for Zara. She had also challenged him to prove it.

*And that's what I'm doing. Proving that I can be more than enough of a parent for Zara.*

Letting Zara's nanny walk away had to be done, no matter how panicked he felt in doing this alone.

Gulping, he hoped this went well and cleared his throat.

"Zara? Can you look up at me, sweetheart?"

She pulled back but kept her small hands latched onto his shoulders. She sat on his lap, looking smaller now that her bottom lip trembled and her eyes and lashes were darker for her tears.

"Why are you crying?"

He'd woken up to her sobbing in Maryan's arms. It was a startling sight to open one's eyes to. Naturally, he'd immediately asked for answers. But he realized snapping at Maryan wasn't fair. She hadn't made him sleepy. He hadn't thought a nap would make him miss a crucial moment relating to Zara. It had, though, and now he hadn't even had the forethought to ask Maryan to catch him up to speed.

Zara sniffed, her head lowering, eyes downcast.

"I can't help you if you don't tell me." Softening his voice, he then added, "I know it's hard, and I can't promise that I'll be able to fix whatever's bothering you, but I'd like to try."

Zara's chin wobbled, and her sniffling grew louder.

He resisted the impatience rising. Remembering that this was a new experience for her in some ways, he tempered the need to rush her through to an explanation. After all, she was ripped away from her mom and home in LA, and she'd been too young to recall living her early life in Istanbul with him and Salma. He couldn't assume any part of this long-distance change was easy on her.

Eventually his forbearance was rewarded with a response.

"My best friends forgot about me."

Why hadn't he thought of that earlier as being a problem? *She's seven!* Friends were at the top of her list of values at that age. What child wanted to be pulled away from their friends?

In a whisper, she said, "I called them and they didn't call me back."

"Was it late for them when you called?"

Zara snapped her head up for a spirited headshake. "I know the time is different here. Maryan told me."

He suspected her brilliant nanny would. Maryan wouldn't have let Zara assume her friends were ignoring her for a simple fact such as time zones.

"Okay, so why do you think they didn't answer your call?"

Zara knit her brows, her consternation carrying into her voice. "I don't know. They don't like me anymore?"

"Did they like you before you left?"

"Yes. They threw me a party. Maryan helped them surprise me, and Mommy brought me to the party, and everyone jumped out with *confeffi*."

"Confetti," he softly amended. "And?"

"And we had cupcakes and cookies. Then we played games like capture the flag and freeze tag, and we pinned a sparkly horn on a unicorn!" Zara regaled him for a bit, painting a picture of that afternoon in sunny Los Angeles, one of her last among friends and family.

*And Maryan.*

Maryan had been by her side then and she still was for now.

He'd thought he was grateful to her before, but that sensation intensified into a hot, bright point that tore open an ache inside him to see her.

Nearly breathless by the end of her story, Zara looked…happier.

That happiness dimmed when she seemed to remember why she was in his lap. Dropping her head, she muttered, "But now they hate me."

"No one hates you," he assured her.

"How do you know?" she shouted. One stern

look from him and she sulked again, mumbling, "Sorry, Daddy. Maryan says I shouldn't yell when I'm angry."

"She's right. *But* I also understand you're upset right now."

She bobbed her head and sniffled.

He embraced her for a moment, letting the sadness be what it was. His mother had taught him that life skill. Sometimes a low mood was just that and nothing more. Chemicals in the brain acting funky. A bad day spoiling a week or more. Most times it passed, and he knew with Zara that it would. But he had to help her through it, and the first step was showing her how to be proactive about her problems.

"When was the last time you spoke to your mom?"

"She left me a voice message yesterday. Maryan played it for me before bed."

His heart did a jig at the mention of her nanny. It had been doing that too much lately.

"Why don't we give your mom a video call later? We can ask her about your friends."

Zara's shy smile told him that she was in, but he teased her.

"Is that a 'yes'?" He tickled her sides.

She shrieked into laughter, the peals of joy floating up into the perfectly cloudless sky. He wrapped her in a bear hug and hauled her up into his arms, her legs dangling around his sides. To see her smiling again meant more to him than he'd ever thought because he had put the smile there on her face. It was a sign that he'd done the right thing by bringing her to live with him.

"Why don't we go find Maryan?" he suggested.

Zara nodded, her enthusiasm for her nanny more innocent than the heated excitement rippling over him whenever he thought of Maryan.

Faisal had their picnic packed up in the backpack slung over his shoulders. Zara skipped by his side, more carefree after their little heart-to-heart. She spied her nanny first and tugged at his hand to get him to move faster.

Maryan was watching tourists and Turkish citizens streaming toward the Çamlıca Mosque, her back facing them.

She turned when Zara called her name.

"Hello," she said simply, her gaze flitting from him to Zara, and he guessed as to why when her expressive dark eyebrows furrowed closer. She couldn't mask her worry for his daughter. And given that he'd sent her away when Zara had still been upset, he realized he needed to fill her in on what happened. Though that would have to wait until they were alone.

"Is this all of the masjid, Daddy?" Zara asked,

using the Arabic word he'd just taught her for the mosque. She didn't hold a trace of sadness in her innocent expression. Only curiosity gazed up at him. Faisal was relieved to see she was back to her normal self.

"The masjid is one part. There's an art gallery, a library and a museum." And an unencumbered view to the Bosporus that he wanted to show them.

"It's so big! Is it the biggest masjid ever? The biggest in the whole world?"

Zara's barrage of questions lightened his heart as usual. Answering her calmly, he flickered glances at Maryan and found her watching them. Surprised to feel an insistent tug of attraction for her in the moment, he concentrated on Zara and decided to untangle his complicated emotions later.

But it wasn't long before Zara pointed to the nonfigurative sculptures in the mosque's expansive courtyard, where other children played.

"Can I go play over there?" she asked.

Faisal nodded, and she wrapped her arms around his legs for a quick hug before doing the same to Maryan and rushing off.

"Walk, please, Zara," Maryan called after her, shading her eyes from the sun and watching Zara move farther away from them.

It left him and Maryan to stroll the courtyard of the newly built mosque.

Since it wasn't a Friday, the holiest day of the week for Muslims, the grand mosque wasn't packed to its capacity of sixty thousand. Still, there were enough tourists and visitors in the courtyard for Faisal to guide Maryan to a quieter section of the mosque's grounds while they watched Zara play. They stood outside the shade of the grand mosque with its domes, half domes and six minarets. Maryan gasped pleasingly at the sight of the city below the valley. He'd shown her Istanbul from many heights now. From his home, Galata Tower and Çamlıca Hill, and now from the mosque. It was what he had promised her: a tour of Istanbul. Taking her to his favorite places in his beloved city was only one small way he could thank her for everything she'd done for Zara up to that point.

*Everything she continued to do.*

All that was left was to thank her in person.

"She's feeling better as you might have noticed." Faisal gazed around Maryan to where Zara had found a group of kids her age to play with. Smiling from a rush of fatherly pride, he reported, "She misses her friends."

"Yes, she does," Maryan agreed. She folded her arms, the gesture more protective than defensive. Casting a look backward at Zara as well, she said, "She's young. It's going to be harder for her to adjust, but she'll make new friends soon enough. She's more resilient than I ever was."

That was an interesting way to put it. He cocked his head, intrigued to know what had caused the melancholy in her voice.

"What do you mean?" he asked.

Maryan snapped her head to him, her pleated brow and frown touched by bafflement. As though she were only piecing it together right then that she'd spoken aloud. And that she wasn't alone when she had.

A shutter rattled in place over her open features. "It's nothing."

"It sounded like *something*." He hoisted the rucksack full of their picnic essentials higher onto his back. "Does this have to do with your family?" She'd mentioned they lived apart from her. The Somali diaspora had scattered many families, rending them apart. It hadn't occurred to him until that moment that she could be a victim of this dispersion. His heart pulled out its next few beats distressingly sharp.

She stroked her tongue over her bottom lip, watching him with a wary slant to her eyes.

Seeing as he couldn't wipe all her worries away with a flick of his wrist, Faisal tried the next best thing.

"I told you my parents left Somalia three decades ago. They were fleeing the civil war and wanted a better life for me." He was turning thirty-eight next month, and a quick calculation reminded him he'd been Zara's age when he'd fled their homeland. No more than seven or eight when he had lost everything he knew and had it replaced with the place he now called home. "It was hard at first. I didn't speak Turkish and my English wasn't good, yet my parents enrolled me in school immediately. They hadn't wanted me to fall behind on my studies. It took some getting used to, a new life here in Istanbul. That's why I know it'll be challenging for Zara."

For a while Maryan remained silent. Then she was quiet for so long, he resigned himself to getting nothing in return for his vulnerability. Not that he'd expected her to reciprocate.

*Still, it would have been nice to hear from her.*

Surprisingly, she finally dispelled the silence with a breathy sigh.

"My parents sent me away because they couldn't feed the whole family. My father owned a corner store, and he'd taken on too much loan from the bank. It was causing an immense strain on them. Then my aunt Nafisa called my mother and suggested that I live with her and her husband, my uncle Abdi, in California."

"How old were you?"

"Twelve. Old enough to be asked an opinion on whether I wanted to go or stay."

He heard the sharp bite to her words. She'd been hurt by a decision that clearly hadn't been fully hers to make. A choice that had altered her life immensely. It was making more and more sense to him *why* she was fiercely protective of Zara. She was fighting for the little girl she'd been who had no voice.

"To be fair, I didn't tell them how I felt." She spoke quietly, a decibel above a whisper if it could be called that. Lowering her arms, she huffed a brisk sigh and angled her head to the sky, her chest rising and falling with her even breathing. "At the time I couldn't think but how selfish it was to speak of my own feelings. My younger brothers and sisters needed my help. That was how I saw it. That, and my parents were relying on me to do something they couldn't do themselves. *They* had to stay behind and care for my siblings, and I had to go."

"Still, it's okay to feel hurt, too."

Maryan slowly lowered her head, blinking the sorrow clear from her eyes.

He knew she was done when she steered the conversation back to Zara.

"For someone who was so sure he couldn't do this on his own, you handled that well."

A blush brightened his face, her compliment

lighting up places he didn't know could be lit. "I understand why she's upset. I'd be, too, if I were in her position right now."

"It's good for her to know that she can talk to you when she's feeling down."

"I know that. I'm also well accustomed to sadness." Given how he'd been raised, he had to be. He hadn't thought he was going to tell Maryan this, as she'd be gone in another week, but he was opening his mouth and talking faster than his brain was processing. "My mom lives with depression."

Maryan didn't say anything, and it was different from what he was used to. Usually, the few people he'd told in the past tripped and tumbled over themselves to try to fill the air with condolences, apologizing as though they'd been responsible for his mother's mental health turn. It was the strangest response. But apparently the most natural or obvious one.

It wasn't helpful, though. None of those people had stuck around by his side.

Salma had been one of them. Like most of the women he'd dated, she'd listened, gone through her rote sympathy, and moved on to the glitzier parts of what his wealth could offer her. Such as access to an elite nightlife and a leg up in networking to expand her career. They'd gone after him for his money. His chest pulsed around the spectral dagger stabbing his heart and hammering the hilt to drive the pain home. He struggled to speak around the emotional suffering.

"My mom's one of the strongest people I know. My father comes in a close second."

"She sounds inspirational. They both do."

Faisal smiled, his pride for his parents rivaling that for Zara. He could talk about them for ages. But he spared Maryan the boringness of it. "She's the reason I'm successful today. When I couldn't kick this idea of starting my own business and, seeing as my parents knew a thing or two about being entrepreneurs, I'd gone to them for advice. It was my mother who suggested I go for it. She never liked it when my sister and I held ourselves back from achieving whatever we set our minds to, not especially when her depression was stronger. She talked my father into early retirement. They sold the bakery and invested half of its sale in my company. All without my knowledge or input. They knew I'd stop them because I wasn't convinced that I would be fortunate in my endeavor."

"They believed in you and your vision."

He liked that Maryan got that. And it reminded him of what she'd said the day she arrived in Istanbul, about how she trusted in his ability to raise Zara alone. She had repeated herself at the bazaar a few days ago. His family knew him.

They loved him. Their support meant the world, and he didn't take it for granted, but he expected it.

*Because that was what family was. A steadfast support unit.*

Unlike his family, Maryan didn't owe him her encouragement.

She'd given it freely.

Faisal pulled a hard swallow. "I never did get to thank you."

"For?" She raised her brows, looking appropriately perplexed.

"I'd given you reason not to trust Zara's care to me." He'd arrived late to the airport, and late to the bazaar. He had confessed about his fear of being a single dad when he'd been a bachelor for too long. He'd been the kind of bachelor who'd lived and seen many parties in his lifetime and all the sin that came with it. Showing her what the media thought of him as a so-called playboy had taken courage because…

*I care what she thinks of me.*

Despite falsely convincing himself he didn't at first.

Faisal couldn't say what it was he felt around Maryan, but it was harder to remember why bottling his emotions was the best recourse for so very long.

Feeling his throat closing from a sudden spike

in anxiety, he babbled out the rest of what he wanted to tell her. "It might not seem like much, but to me, it was kindness. A kindness I didn't feel I deserved at the time because I couldn't see where the trust in me was coming from. Now that I do, it means even more."

Maryan's lips parted slightly, presumably to reply.

He tensed his muscles in anticipation.

Whatever her response might have been was swallowed up by the call to prayer, the undiluted sound of the muezzin's voice reverberating through the courtyard. The crowds thronging around the mosque split into two groups, those who weren't religiously observing and remained unruffled by the call, and those who hadn't entered the mosque earlier but were now moving toward it to observe prayer indoors. They fell into the latter group.

He'd be separated from Maryan now.

"I'll need my hijab, and Zara's, too."

He held still while she stepped behind him, opened the backpack, and rummaged through for the shawls they'd need to enter the mosque. She looked the same with a hijab on. Just as beautiful in the pearl-and-lace headscarf as she was without it.

"Is it on crooked?" Maryan's hands rose automatically to her head to right an imagined wrong.

And he was to blame because he'd been gawking at her rudely.

Embarrassed, he shook his head quickly. Too quickly. "No!" On his second attempt, he managed a more subtle, albeit hoarse, "No, you look…perfect."

It was her turn to color from shocked to abashed. She looked as flustered as he felt.

Zara raced over to them, her cheeks glowing from her run, her eyes wide with wonder. "Daddy, Maryan, can we go inside the big masjid now?"

Maryan helped Zara wrap her hijab, then pulled the small girl into a side hug and smiled quickly at him before turning them toward the mosque for their tour. As they walked before him, he noticed they appeared like a family.

*One big happy family.*

Stricken by how perfectly normal that thought felt to him, he rid it from his mind and forced it from his thundering heart. Because as much as he liked Maryan, and as wholly unlike the women he'd been romantically engaged with as she was, she couldn't mean anything more to him.

For that he would have to risk his heart.

And he'd decided love wasn't worth its weight in joy *and* pain.

## CHAPTER SIX

TWO DAYS LATER, Faisal arrived home late, exhausted from working overtime but his spirits soaring at the thought that he'd be seeing Maryan and Zara soon. He hadn't liked breaking their plans today to tour more of Istanbul, but he'd had no choice in the matter. His board had called for an emergency meeting. They'd had questions about his leadership and direction in steering investors. Springing it on him hadn't made it any easier. Though in the end he'd been able to talk them into his confidence again, the onus fell on him to handle his board's fragile trust delicately. They wouldn't give him a second chance to secure this oil and natural gas partnership.

Groaning softly, he keyed in the pass code to his security gate when his driver pulled up. Faisal thanked his driver from the back seat as the car slowed and parked in his drive. Instead of heading up above his garage to his apartment for a much-needed workout, shower and change of clothes, he walked toward the main house.

Funny how nothing had changed at work. He was still flogging this same horse.

*And yet everything has changed at home.*

He no longer arrived at his house and anticipated spending the short hours of night into dawn trapped in his office, where he'd squeeze in more work. Nor was he answering any of the invites from his usual social circle to meet up at their typical haunts. He'd pushed all that aside these days, knowing full well that he would be winding down the evening with Maryan and Zara. They'd taken over his life in a way that had him smiling more and more. Even now he felt his lips spreading synchronously to the warmth pouring out from the center of his chest. If he'd gulped a big cup of black coffee, he would feel the same lively jolt.

The jolt peaked when he opened the front door. Voices rang out from deeper inside the house. It sounded like Maryan and Zara weren't alone.

"Maryan? Zara?"

He followed the voices to the kitchen.

Maryan and Zara were there, along with his diligent housekeeper, Lalam.

Zara noticed him first, her loud, cheery, "Daddy!" grabbing the attention of Maryan and Lalam.

He approached them slowly, curious as to why their faces and clothes were covered in flour.

Zara appeared the messiest, her small cheeks caked white from the flour, and even the ends of her braids were chalky white from the stuff.

"What are you baking?" he asked, his intrigue intensified.

"Maryan's teaching Lalam how to make Somali candy, and I'm helping."

"Somali candy?" He looked to Maryan for clarification.

*"Kac kac,"* she said, wiping her hands with a tea towel. A towel she soaked the end of before swiping it over Zara's cheeks. She cleaned her up as best as she could, but the damage required Zara to shower. She'd need to wash the flour from her hair.

"We're not done yet, Daddy. You have to wait to eat it," Zara was telling him.

"I'd like that." He hadn't had *kac kac* in a long while. Less of a candy and more doughnut, the soft, subtly sweet Somali fritters had been a staple in his house, especially during Ramadan.

"You look tired," Maryan remarked, her hands kneading into her portion of the dough. Beside her Lalam rolled out a second portion. Zara clung to the edge of the counter and stood on tiptoes to watch them work. It was a wonder how she managed to get the most flour on her when she wasn't doing much.

Scooping Zara up and helping her to a seat on

the counter, Faisal said, "That's putting it mildly. I've certainly had better days. But it's nice to see friendly faces." He tickled his daughter then, and she broke into a fit of breathless giggles.

Maryan was frowning at him when he glanced in her direction. "You've got flour on you now, too."

"I guess I do." He regarded his shirt front and navy blue herringbone suit jacket. Flour dusted parts of his sleeves. It hadn't occurred to him that it'd be a problem. It wasn't like he didn't have a walk-in closet full of similar-looking costly suits. Zara's laughter and happiness were worth so much more. "I think we'll all need to clean up after this."

"Actually, I'm almost done here. I'll take Zara up for a bath."

Lalam stopped Maryan. "I will help Zara." The housekeeper slipped off her apron and lifted Zara off the counter. They left the kitchen hand in hand, Zara still wearing her apron and her flour-caked braids bouncing up and down as she skipped beside Lalam. Their carefree chattering floated farther away until silence filled the kitchen.

"Isn't it Lalam's day off?" he asked, shrugging off his suit jacket and rolling up his sleeves.

"It is, but she came in to bake with us."

"I see. Who taught you to make *kac kac*?" He

washed his hands at the sink and dried them before taking up the dough that Lalam had been rolling. Feeling Maryan's questioning gaze, he laughed softly and said, "Don't worry. I know what I'm doing. I won't make the dough too thin." He rolled precisely, pressing on the rolling pin lightly and evening the dough to a quarter-inch thickness. Just about the right size for it to puff nicely in the frying oil.

"I could ask you that question."

He laughed again. "My parents owned a bakery, remember?"

She flashed him a small smile. "My *hooyo* taught me."

Faisal wasn't surprised to hear her mother had passed on the essential skill. In Somalia, women handled much of the cookery. It was thought to prepare a young girl for when she was old enough to be married and manage her own household. His parents had raised him in Turkey, though, and they'd expected him to know his way around the kitchen as much as his sister, Yasmin, did.

Not that this was about him or his opposition to patriarchal society's inherent sexism.

Anything he learned about Maryan was good information in his books.

"Your mom must have been a great teacher."

"She was." Maryan pressed her dough between her hands and the counter, flattening it into a round shape before accepting the rolling pin he passed to her and rolling it as he'd done. She worked faster than him and achieved the same result. Clearly, she'd practiced more than he had.

She swiped flour onto her cheek, the curly black strand of hair she'd been trying to unstick from her face persistently remaining fixed to her. She had her hair in a messy bun, yet she still was attractive to him. Her beauty was unblemished by the flour spotting her cheek and the sheen of perspiration making her forehead glow. He wished he felt differently about her. His life was complicated as it was without throwing in the odd thoughts he'd had lately of family, love and romance.

None of it worked for him before. He'd tried family with Salma when she'd sprung her pregnancy on him, and then he'd depleted his endurance for dating seriously—with all intent to marry someday—on his heartless past partners. Without his money, he'd have meant nothing to them. It was tiring to pretend like the vultures hadn't chased him out of the dating scene. He'd gone from being hopeful to a cynic in a short time after hitting his first million. And for years he had been happy to date for pleasure instead. One night or a few months, it didn't matter because it never lasted long-term. Salma had given him pause only because their short-term pleasure had resulted in the miracle of new life.

When she arrived in the world, Zara held his heart alone. His adorable little girl.

Considering his rocky history with romance, it sat oddly with him whenever his eyes strayed to Maryan. It was a hard feeling to fight, too. She captivated him. He had this strange compelling urge to watch her work the dough evenly on the counter.

She wore a pale green petal-sleeved tee and black jeans that molded to her thick thighs and shapely legs.

He tracked his eyes up to find her looking back, her lips tilting downward.

Groping for words, he ended up bumbling, "You're good at being a nanny, good at baking, what else can you do?"

"Yoga."

"Yoga?" he parroted, images of her in fitted workout gear flitting through his mind and warming his body. He wished she hadn't answered. He *wished* he hadn't asked. Harmless as it sounded, it was wreaking havoc with his senses. A familiar yearning heated his groin. Disgust curled above his lust, rising like froth to the top of his simmering emotions. He'd been raised better. Objectifying her felt…perverted. Disrespectful. Wrong.

It was worse because he knew nothing more could come of it were they to fall into bed together.

And Maryan came across as faithful. The type who'd want chocolate hearts and commitment, and flowers and wedding vows. Family.

The things he couldn't give her.

He didn't want to give *anyone*. At least that was what he'd believed until she came into his world.

"I relax with yoga. What do you do to unwind?"

Her question pinged off him. "What?"

She paused in rolling the dough. "I asked what your hobbies are. Work doesn't count."

This he could answer. Chuckling, he replied, "I read when I can."

"I've seen your library. Zara loves the fairy-tale collection you chose for her."

"They were the ones my parents used to read to me and my sister when they weren't telling us the old Somali folktales."

"The fox and the hyena?" She grinned knowingly.

He laughed. "I think it's a rite of passage."

"They were violent, though. Humorous, but more Grimm than Disney."

"Good point. It won't hurt Zara to grow a little older to hear them."

"What else?" she encouraged, brushing flour

from her hands and reaching for a paring knife. She sliced the dough into quarters. Each piece was then transferred to a clean, dry plate.

"Well, you've met my Turkish drama addiction."

They'd been going through his collection of Turkish films every night. Action-packed thrillers, to mysteries, and even the occasional romance. Zara never lasted for very long, her bedtime early. It left him and Maryan to watch more of the films together. He'd grown to cherish the time more than he felt he ought to. Attachment was a dangerous thing.

"Do you watch Salma's films?" Maryan asked.

He'd told her about Salma beginning her acting career in small Turkish roles. She picked up the language quickly when she'd been living with him.

"Only small clips, but I'm saving them for Zara."

"She loves watching her mom on TV," she approved.

"I bet she does." He checked the fryer, seeing that she'd had the oil changed and readied for the fritters. That time allowed him to sort and organize his thinking. "One thing that we'd agreed on is to keep Zara in both of our lives. I'd never hold her back from her mother."

"It's a solid rule for co-parenting." Maryan

rolled and sliced her second piece of dough. She had one left, and she was making quick work in completing it.

He found tongs for her to use. Fetched a cooling rack and cookie pan to drain the fritters once they were done. He did all that he could do until he ran out of errands to run around the kitchen. She noticed, too, her eyes having followed him while he'd moved around his kitchen and helped her in his own way.

"She thinks pretty highly of you, too."

"Does she?" A sense of unease shivered through him. He didn't want to stand there and talk about Salma, not when he kept stealing glances at Maryan's lips and wondering what they might feel like against his. The air in the kitchen was growing to be stiflingly hot—

"Why aren't you together?"

A coldness showered over him, her query the trigger to the ice flooding his veins and the frost seeping into his heart.

It wasn't her fault. She didn't understand how loaded the question was, how complicated the response to it would be if he allowed it. He stuck to the simplest answer. "We aren't together because we don't want to be. And we didn't want to pretend to be, either."

"*Do* you ever plan to marry someday? Give Zara a stepmother? Maybe brothers and sisters?"

She plated the last of the dough and switched on the fryer. Working and talking and avoiding his eyes all at the same time. "Billionaires are a catch, aren't they?"

"Funny thing about money. It attracts all sorts of people." And it was difficult to distinguish between who was with him for his wealth and who wanted him.

None of which he said aloud to her, fearing he'd come across pathetic. Like she'd have any sympathy for him.

*The poor billionaire can't reel in a serious relationship. Boo-hoo*, he thought derisively.

Tired of the spotlight being on him, Faisal shifted gears and focus.

"And you? Has your ex jaded you beyond the point of no return?"

Maryan should have known. She couldn't even fault him for asking, not after she'd pried into his love life. It didn't stop her from stalling with her response. Luckily the fryer was ready. She popped in a few pieces of dough, the crackle and scent of fried oil diffusing in the kitchen. It took all of thirty seconds. Seconds she relished before she faced the one-man firing squad.

Faisal's good looks dulled some of the pain murmuring through her heavy chest.

She breathed in deep, expelling as much of the

negativity as she could. What she couldn't shake off she carried into her story.

"I wouldn't call it 'no return.' Just a long, *long* vacation from the warfare of dating."

He snorted. "That bad?"

Hassan's betrayal had cut deeply. But he hadn't been her first boyfriend. She'd dated duds like him through high school and college. Enough men to know she had a type. A rough-around-the-edges but charming type. Hassan had been that. His confidence and winsome personality had lured her in. He seemed a perfect fit at her aunt and uncle's restaurant. Working his way up from busing to the kitchen. When their old sous-chef retired, Maryan talked her aunt and uncle into taking a chance on Hassan.

She'd liked him.

But it had taken a while—nearly most of their three years of dating—for her to realize she didn't *love* him.

Breaking up felt appropriate. Even the kind thing to do. She'd thought Hassan understood why she had to do it. She never would have guessed he was angry enough at her to steal from the restaurant and flee before he was caught.

*The two-faced idiot.*

Maryan turned the fritters over in the crack-ling oil, tucking her anger away where it couldn't leave her unguarded in front of Faisal. For some reason still unknown to her, she didn't want him to see her weakened. She liked that he thought her strong, a fierce lioness, and someone who'd protect his daughter to the ends of the earth. It was the exact opposite of how she saw herself when she looked in the mirror. After all, to be strong meant to be willing to fight for one's values…and she hadn't done that. With her parents, she'd allowed them to do as they wished, and it resulted in her being shipped off to grow up without her family. Then Hassan used and abused her trust, robbing her and her family blind, and leaving her feeling like his accomplice. She'd brought him into the confidence of her aunt and uncle. They had relied on him, and only because they placed their faith on her word.

If Maryan hadn't vouched for him, her aunt and uncle wouldn't have taken the hit to their finances. Once she was done in Istanbul, she owed it to them to return and help them earn what they'd lost and assuage her persisting guilt.

She brooded and nearly missed the pastries turning the right shade of golden brown.

"Here." Faisal held a spider skimmer under her nose.

She'd completely forgotten she would need the long-handled spoon to fish the fritters out.

Their hands touched when he passed her the handle. She froze at the same time he did. They stared at each other, and then she took hold of the kitchen tool and scooped the fritters out into the safety of the colander at the end of the handle.

As she added the second batch of *kac kac*, Maryan sensed Faisal's eyes on her.

He reached over to the freshly baked fritters. "A *kac kac* for your thoughts?"

"Careful, they're hot," she warned, her sternness melting when he grabbed a fritter, bit into it and groaned his pleasure, his eyes fluttering shut. She didn't think eating could conjure such a sexual picture. And yet Faisal had her imagining a dimly lit bedroom, slippery silk sheets and heated limbs intertwining in passion.

Maryan blushed furiously when he opened his eyes and stared at her with an altogether different hunger.

The emotion flashed briefly in his half-lidded gaze before blinking out of existence.

"Damn. I think this might be the best *kac kac* I've had."

"You think?" she taunted, watching him demolish the fried delicacy. Surprised she could flirt when he left her feeling breathless physically and emotionally.

He smirked and licked his fingers slowly until they were crumb-free. "It's definitely the best I've had."

A pleasurable shudder rippled through her at

his double entendre. Flushed all over, it felt like, she cleared her throat and muttered, "Thank you."

She popped the latest batch of fritters out and placed the last set into the cooling oil. Cranking up the heat slightly, she glanced up to his intense stare.

"I'm sorry to have asked about your ex."

Maryan shrugged. "It's only fair. I asked you about Salma." She'd done more than ask; she'd poked and prodded him for information, convincing herself it was to help Zara when she wanted the details for herself just as much.

"Still, I didn't mean to make you sad."

He'd noticed the change in her mood then. What he didn't have was the full story to work with, otherwise he would know that nothing he'd asked had deliberately instigated her turn in mood.

Before she thought too much on it, she said, "He stole from us."

Faisal's jaw hardened visibly, his face transforming into steel.

"It wasn't that much." A few thousand out of pocket. The restaurant was doing well enough for the stolen money not to cause a massive problem. It was just the principle. The fact that they'd been betrayed by Hassan. Taken for fools.

*I'd been the fool.*

And now she felt foolish when she heard it said

aloud. "He didn't like it when I broke up with him. I'd thought that it was mutual…"

She'd been wrong.

"How is that your fault?"

"I should have figured he was upset."

Faisal pulled in a loud breath, his hand quicker to the spider strainer on the counter. He flipped the fritters, saving them from being scorched on one side. Frown in place, he looked at her. "You're shouldering blame senselessly."

She sputtered, bouncing between whether she should be annoyed he'd butt in with his opinion, or relieved that he could see how ludicrously tough she was being on herself.

In the end it was near impossible to remain irritated when he plucked a fritter from the plate and waved it in front of her face.

"Indulge yourself," he urged. "I can't think of anyone who's more deserving of a treat right now."

She accepted the soft fried dough, gaining immediate comfort from biting into it.

He snagged another one, too.

"Feeling better?" he asked her when they finished eating in silence.

"A little." She was feeling silly that he even had to ask. Sighing, she said, "It's a trust issue. I trusted my parents, and it brought me to America. I trusted my ex, and he stole from my family."

Maryan let that truth settle over her. She'd thought it plenty of times before. Registering Faisal's empathetic smile wedged open room for growth beyond that circular thinking. Like she'd found in him a kindred spirit.

"Trust is fickle," he agreed gruffly.

"Mine is close to nonexistent."

Rather than ridiculing her for being dramatic, he dipped his head. "On that, we can agree."

"Are we talking from experience?" She quirked an eyebrow, checking on the slowly frying fritters.

"Yeah."

His monosyllabic response should have persuaded her away from the subject, but she recalled how he'd lifted her up when she had been hard on herself. And when he turned his back on the plate of deep-fried pastries, she had to speak up.

"Bad breakup, too?"

"A string of them, actually."

Her mouth flopped open. She should have known. Faisal was hot. His model-worthy good looks had to be reeling in all sorts of interest. Mostly her surprise was because he'd had more bad luck it seemed than she did. *Not* that she likely dated as much as he had, or that any of her dates were internationally renowned like his former partners were. Really, there was very little comparison to go on between the two of them. Worlds apart as they were.

"I mentioned money being a problem."

He had.

"It's a real thing. There are loads of deceptive people who would date me for my net worth. Loads who have."

"Sorry."

"Then there's the paranoia." His brows scrunched, deep brackets framing his scowling mouth, his eyes looking ahead but his features revealing the pain his dating experience had taught him. "The overthinking is the worst part of it. It's ruined a date or two...or three. I keep asking myself if I'm who they want, or if I'm a package deal. And if they'll take the money someday and run."

"Have you tried dating online? It'd be easier to hide your identity. At least until you could get to know someone."

He shook his head and didn't look like her suggestion made him any happier. "It won't change that there will always be a part of me that questions, wonders, *doubts*. And I can't enter anything serious and long-term with that hanging over me. It wouldn't be fair. I wouldn't be true to myself."

She pulled the fritters out one by one, flicked off the fryer and closed its lid.

"Guess we're both jaded in similar ways."

"Trust," he echoed her unspoken thought, his laugh raspy and joyless. "Where does that leave us?"

"Clinging to hope?" she offered.

Faisal tipped his head to the side, his eyes boring into her, face closed to any emotion. "How old are you?"

"Why?"

"You look young enough for hope." He raked a hand through his silky-looking black curls, the longer ones on top clinging to his fingers and distracting her more than they should. His huff of indignation grounded her. "But I'm thirty-eight next month. Old enough to be worrying my mother that I'll never properly settle down and give her another grandchild."

"I'll be twenty-seven this September."

"I'd have guessed your mid-twenties. I was right, then. Young enough for things like hope."

She oscillated from flattered to puzzled, to finally landing on insatiably intrigued.

"Where are you going with this?"

"Don't you want to get married? Have kids?" He answered her question with a question, but it was a *good* one. Annoyingly so.

"Possibly. Someday. Though not anytime soon."

"Because you have plans after you head home. For your aunt and uncle's restaurant."

She nodded. "That, and I'll likely take a second job."

"Where?"

"Before Salma hired me, I used to teach cooking classes at my neighborhood's community center." Maryan smiled at the fond memories of working alongside her students of all ages. Young and old, novice and aficionado, and from a variety of backgrounds. Everyone had shared one thing in common: a passion for making tasty meals. Reminiscing had her thinking of her aunt and uncle and her obligations back home.

"They've been talking about renovating the restaurant's dining room for a while now. But that means they'll have to close shop temporarily." And they were already a little tight with money after her ex's stupid stunt. That was where the job at the community center would come in handy. Maryan's boss had liked her, and she'd left on good footing. She made a mental note to reach out for job prospects soon as she returned to California.

Which was sooner than she liked…

*But it's not like any of this with Faisal and Zara was permanent.*

"That explains a lot." Faisal lifted the plate of fritters, holding it between them when he angled his body to face her fully. "These are phenomenally good. Have you ever considered opening your own business?"

"A bakery, you mean?"

"Sure," he said, all lopsided smile and irresistible charm. "I could be your first investor. You could pay me in baked goods."

She swatted his hand before he reached another fried pastry. "Save some for Zara."

"No fair. You two cleared out my baklava stash."

Noting her confusion, he traded the plate of pastry to open a top cabinet and pull down a nearly empty container.

Maryan recognized it and realized where he was going with this. "My stash. You've demolished it."

"We didn't 'demolish' anything. We've had a few," she lied.

Faisal shook the nearly empty container at her.

"Okay, we ate a little more than that, but there wasn't much left in there."

Chuckling, he said, "Try harder to convince me."

"First the tea stash, now baklava. This secret snacking is concerning, Faisal."

"Don't turn this around on me." He laughed. "I'll negotiate for another one or two *kac kac* to stock more baklava."

She pretended to think about it before nodding. "You have yourself a deal."

He offered her a hand.

Maryan hesitated a second, and then she grasped his hand, his long, strong fingers holding hers in an even-pressured grip.

Their hands remained clasped longer than necessary.

Longer than she'd have normally liked.

But Faisal had made her feel like she wasn't alone. Like her troubles were his in a way, and she'd come out of this baking and talking feeling lighter, calmer.

*Happier.*

"Maryan." He spoke her name in a breathy whisper; a reverence pulsed from those two syllables. So much so that it sounded less like her name and more like a prayer. She shivered visibly, unable to help the reaction. Her body temperature rose when he closed the short gap between them and his hand brushed up her arm before moving to cup her too-warm cheek. It was a simple touch that set off a firework of desire in her.

"Thank you for listening. For asking. For pushing to know."

He spoke her mind. Those were the exact words she wished to utter to him. And she would have, had she had a voice to do it with.

His next breath was drawn out, the heat of it brushing her cheek when he planted a quick kiss there.

She stood frightfully still, the pressure of his soft mouth, the emotion behind the gesture, forcing open an ocean's worth of yearning for him. When he slowly drew his head up, almost reluctantly, Maryan made her choice.

Or maybe he'd made it first, and she went along for the ride.

Because when his eyes regarded her, and his face pushed in closer again, their noses brushing, she pulled up onto her toes and connected their lips in an intimate play of his chaste kiss on her cheek. A hunger accentuated their lip-lock. It colored the moan rumbling through his chest and the heated press of their bodies as he backed her into the opposite counter.

Resurfacing for air was expected but unwanted.

Maryan would've gladly allowed Faisal to steal another kiss and rob her of breath again. A clanging alertness took hold of her when he growled, "Maryan," and splayed his heavy, warm hands on her hips.

This time she knew who made the decision for them.

She pushed him away first. Gently, pleadingly. She didn't have the strength to do it twice.

"We *can't*." And they really couldn't. They had to think of Zara. What would she wonder if she caught them kissing?

*And I'm leaving in a week.*

A week wasn't a good enough reason to jump into bed with the first good-looking billionaire who swept her off her feet. Chemistry or no chemistry, sleeping with Faisal would be a stupid and dangerous move. Stupid because there was no chance it would become a meaningful relationship, and dangerous for the very same reason.

She backed away, her shaking hands giving up on untying her apron.

Abandoning the kitchen, she hightailed it to her room and didn't look back until she closed her door.

She counted the seconds that lapsed from the time she left him.

When no knock came from the other side and no footsteps down the hall, she pressed a hand to her thumping heart and analyzed what happened downstairs with Faisal.

He'd kissed her.

Correction: *they* had kissed.

She'd been an active participant in it. That, and she couldn't kid herself that she hadn't thought of kissing him before then.

As Maryan stood there, her body more alive

in that second than it ever was, two things were clearer now about her and Faisal. Their hearts were both closed off to love, and their attraction was a potent force of nature that went against everything she thought she could feel with another human being before.

# CHAPTER SEVEN

"Tonight's perfect. I'll see you both then."

Faisal pulled his Bluetooth from his ear and dropped it on top of the blueprint of an oil rig overtaking his office desk. Rukiya had been sitting across from him; her eyes, glued to her tablet, sprang up to him as soon as he ended his phone call. She looked as he'd felt before he had taken the call: nervous.

Thankfully he had good news for her.

"They're willing to discuss our original terms for the partnership over dinner."

All wasn't lost after all. The Turkish brothers he'd hoped to partner with were reconsidering their hasty decision not to sign their deal. Faisal's grin edged on manic as he realized what that meant; his board wouldn't have anything to hold over his head, and his company's hard work and effort wouldn't go to waste. Moreover, the people of Somalia stood a chance at being uplifted by this project. Assuming his dinner went smoothly, and everyone walked away happy.

"Shall I look into restaurants?"

"No, they've already made their reservations." Which was more than fine by him. He had enough on his plate to think about. Zara...

*Maryan and our kiss.*

He'd thought of Zara's nanny plenty since yesterday. Now, nearly twenty-four hours later, Faisal still didn't feel any better about how their explosive brush of intimacy ended. She had run away from him.

*It's not a good sign*, he thought glumly.

And for once he didn't know what to do around a woman.

It wasn't like he had to fight for the attention and affection. Women liked him. He liked them, too, well enough to hook up when he needed an itch scratched. He hadn't had any of them push him away after a kiss.

Or flee from him.

Once again, for what had to be the millionth time, he tripped over that fact and fell flat on his face. All the thinking he'd done left him with no answer to solve the riddle that Maryan had become to him overnight. She was a beautiful enigma. One he wanted to kiss again over and over until they were both breathless.

What wasn't a mystery was their chemistry.

He'd been right about his instinct. They were mutually attracted to each other. It was enough for him to hope by the time they spoke again yesterday's worst parts would have been forgotten. And they'd be speaking sooner as his evening plans were now changed. But first he'd clear his office and end another long day of work.

"Feel free to leave for home, Rukiya. Thank you for staying longer again."

His executive assistant nodded her acknowledgment. "If that's all then," she said, standing. "Have a good night, Mr. Umar, and enjoy your dinner."

Before Rukiya reached the exit of his office, a knock at his door had Faisal calling out, "Come in."

Burak opened the door and remained on the threshold as he explained his presence.

"One of the secretaries has a message for you."

Rukiya managed his messages at her desk primarily. She'd been with him most of the day, researching alternative partners for their foray into the oil and gas industry. Naturally, she appeared clueless when Burak forwarded this news.

"I can look into it," his efficient EA commented.

"That's fine. Have the secretary call my office." When Burak lingered, Faisal asked, "Was there another message you had to deliver?"

Burak flickered his eyes to Rukiya, his expression brightening. "I was on my way out. Shift change in the security office. Would you like a ride home?"

Faisal couldn't see Rukiya's face, but she sounded bashful when she assented, "I'd like that, thank you."

They left together, his office feeling emptier without them.

*Good on them.*

He wished them a peaceful night. They'd done enough for him as it was. Everyone in his company, from his top executives to his middle management and line employees, had striven equally hard for each of their investments. His dream project in Somalia transformed from a personal goal into a community one, shared by his colleagues, employees and investors alike. Any win now would be a win for all of them.

His office landline rang. He answered, knowing it'd be the secretary with his message.

"Mr. Umar, your daughter called."

"My daughter?" Recovering from the surprise, he hurried the secretary off the line politely. Fitting his Bluetooth back in his ear, he pulled his phone from where his suit coat hung on the back of his chair and dialed Maryan.

She answered after only a ring. For that alone he could kiss her. He didn't think he could stand another second of suspense.

"I just heard word that Zara called me."

"Typically, people start with a 'hello' first." Maryan's dry humor warmed his unease. She wouldn't sound so relaxed were Zara in any real danger or harm. He should have known that she would care for his daughter. Maryan might have confused him with her reaction after their steamy kiss, but he was confident in trusting her with Zara's well-being.

"Sorry. I had a long day."

"Will you not be coming home?"

Home. She'd called his place home. It wasn't his imagining. Wiping the burgeoning smile from his face, he said, "I've been invited to dinner to salvage the hope of my company's partnership deal. It's tonight, though."

"That's great news. Sudden, but good."

"It is," he agreed, grinning from ear to ear. He could feel it overtaking his face the second her praise came through the line. "I was calling to let you know I'm on my way now. I know it's late, but is Zara awake?"

"No, sadly. She was calling to ask you to come home to read to her. She prefers your ogre voices over mine."

Their bedtime routine had quickly grown to become his favorite part of the day.

"You can still creep in and kiss her. She's a deep sleeper."

"Good suggestion," he said, his heart galloping now as he stood and cleared his desk. He had one other thing on his mind, and there wasn't a better opportunity than to do it now, when her end of the line grew quiet. "Maryan?"

She hummed. "Yeah?"

"About dinner… Would you want to be my plus-one?"

Faisal's explanation for inviting her was sound.

He didn't want to go alone when everyone else in the dinner party would be coupled up. Saving him from being a fifth wheel, Maryan agreed to the short-notice dinner. It was the kindest thing to do for him.

It wasn't like the sparking, fizzing delight at having been asked was her *only* motivator.

She just had to remember not to be lulled into a delusion. This was a one-off. They weren't dating for real. And it would be easier not to be tempted if the scent of Faisal's cologne weren't so dreamy. Thinking straight was proving improbable when the peppery spice of his aftershave wafted under her nose teasingly throughout the evening. Mostly when he leaned in to check in on her. Fighting against the instinct to draw closer to him, inhale his essence and commit it to memory for when she left Istanbul, Maryan focused on the faces around the table.

Faisal's hosts…and hers as well.

It wasn't long, though, before she was drawn back to him. A moth to a flame. A fly snared in a web. Only instead of the fear of a fly or a moth, every time she looked at him, an undercurrent of immeasurable pleasure overtook her. And in the pleasure, there was an assurance in knowing he hadn't asked anyone else to be his date.

*He kissed me yesterday.*

Naturally she'd thought of their kiss first when he asked her. She had to be realistic, though. For Faisal, finding women and getting them to spend an evening with him surely wasn't a trying task. He could probably do it with his eyes closed.

If his handsome face didn't lure them, then his money. He'd said so himself: he had trouble trusting his romantic partners and questioning their motives for dating him.

Still, even with his reservations, he'd chosen to be with her tonight. Maryan had little doubt he could've found another woman to fill her wedge heels. Had she declined his invitation, he'd likely have gone that route. Replaced her easily.

Her heart felt like it skipped a beat when he glanced at her, his conversation with the two men sitting across the table flowing freely up until that moment. She guessed that he'd seen something on her face.

He stopped talking and turned into her, leaning closer to whisper in Somali, "Are you doing all right?"

The Somali rang to her as more intimate. Mostly as no one else at the table understood them. And there was the bonus of being able to talk freely.

"It's getting late, that's all." The sun had set, but the sky nearer the horizon glowed soft yellows and oranges. It looked more magical from where they were sitting. She hadn't thought a rooftop restaurant could feel very romantic. Certainly not when a chilly breeze kept nipping at her bare shoulders whenever her shawl slipped to her elbows. The floral embroidered cocktail dress was a favorite of hers, and the only thing she considered suitable for a semiformal dinner. But now she wished she'd worn something warmer.

A shiver strummed through her.

"Are you cold?" Faisal pulled his jacket off quicker than she could stop him.

He covered her shoulders, his body heat and cologne blanketing her. It was like he was hugging her.

Blushing when his face remained close to her, she ducked her head and muttered, "Thank you." She kept her head down, unprepared to face the rest of the table but sensing their eyes fixed on her and Faisal. Their attention was warranted. Faisal had introduced her as his daughter's nanny.

Bringing her as his plus-one made enough of a statement. They had to be wondering what a billionaire was doing with an ordinary salaried worker.

Unperturbed, Faisal faced the table and continued his conversation as if it were perfectly normal to drape his jacket over her.

She wondered if that was why he hadn't mentioned their kiss.

*It would make sense, wouldn't it? He's likely kissed many times.*

One kiss with her wasn't an earth-shattering event. Whatever she might think or feel, she had to remember that Faisal was far worldlier than her. Romanticizing a single, inconsequential encounter wouldn't be something he would do.

She barely tasted her dessert after that. The rosewater and lemony flavor of the Turkish delights no longer bloomed as vibrantly on her tongue. It tasted more of its cornstarch dusting than its beautiful flavors and robust chewy texture. She chewed, swallowed, bit and repeated until she drained her pear-shaped glass of traditional Turkish coffee.

The sand-filled pan warming their coffee sat in the middle of the table. It had fascinated her when their waiter joined them and shuffled the sand closer to the sides of the pot with a metal scoop. Faisal had explained that the pan sat over an open flame and gave the waiter complete control over the heat. The coffee would never be too hot or too cool.

Another thing she had to get used to about Turkish coffee: the fine-ground coffee beans were not filtered out of the cup. This method resulted in a thicker, stronger brew.

She gagged on the first sip, admittedly. But by her second cup she felt more like a pro. More like she belonged by Faisal's side, among these beautifully dressed people.

There were four of them. The two Turkish brothers who Faisal mentioned to her. Aydin and Erkin. Erkin was younger and was the other purported playboy seated at their table. Impressively tall, he was also incredibly thin and his face was all bony angles and lines. But his broad smile and booming voice made up for his gaunt, emaciated appearance. His older brother, Aydin, was the traditional-minded brother of the two. Faisal had warned her that Aydin was the one they had to impress. He called the shots when it came to the partnership deal. Shorter than Erkin, Aydin made up for his height difference by perfecting a dour-faced expression that kept her on edge all through dinner. Aydin spent half the evening stroking his long wiry beard thoughtfully, and the other half he spoke in an even tone that masked his true thoughts.

She realized it was a tactic. Acting uninterested when they talked business and carrying that indifference to small talk about the weather, sports games, politics. Faisal mirrored his blasé attitude. It gave her a glimpse into how he'd managed to amass billions in such a short span of time.

There was a seductive power to his no-nonsense voice. An energy that abounded in his every little movement.

She could watch him work all day… He was that magnetizing when he was in his element. He brokered multimillion-dollar deals, negotiated with equally powerful businessmen and looked incredibly sexy when his singular focus and passion collided.

"Maryan?"

Maryan was startled when she heard her name.

She swiped the back of her hand over her mouth for lack of a napkin. Still worrying that she had cornstarch powder dusting her mouth, she faced the woman beside her on the cushioned floor sofa.

Aslihan was one of the two other women at the table. She'd come as Erkin's date. Hatice was Aydin's wife and she sat by her husband. Unlike Hatice, Aslihan was…catty. Maryan had learned why soon after she and Faisal arrived for dinner. Aslihan and Faisal had a past. They'd been neighbors as children before Aslihan and her family had moved to Turkey's capital, Ankara. But Aslihan had to jog Faisal's memory when he hadn't recognized her immediately. She'd been ready to sink her claws into him. Only Maryan's presence had stopped her from it.

Because of that she'd had to deal with Aslihan's passive-aggressive comments most of the night.

Like the one Aslihan uttered right then. "So, how long are you staying in Istanbul, Maryan?"

"I have a week left." One more week with Faisal in his home. Seven days before she had to leave Zara forever and pick up her life in California.

"I suppose you'll miss Faisal's daughter." Aslihan looked past Maryan, presumably to Faisal. She'd been watching him like a hawk stalking its prey all night. The longing in her eyes made it hardest for Maryan, especially as Aslihan was a far better fit for him.

Jealousy dragged its claws over Maryan's insides.

"My job would have ended someday," she said through a gritted-teeth smile. "It's only unfortunate that it's ending sooner." And then because she hated the sting of tears sparking at her eyes, Maryan shoved a bigger piece of Turkish delight in her mouth to keep from answering any more questions.

Aslihan took the hint and struck up a chat with Hatice.

Eventually the evening wound down, and Aydin and Hatice stood for their departure.

Faisal held a hand down to Maryan. "We'll walk them out," he said with a coaxing smile.

She slipped her hand in his, not caring that he assumed she wanted to go with him. The excitement at touching him again coiling electric pleasure through her heated blood.

Aydin's brother Erkin waved them off. He had asked for a hookah to be brought to the table. He smoked from the single-stem pipe, the fumes of the shisha rising over their heads. Aslihan remained seated as well, her envious eyes narrowed and pinned on Maryan and Faisal's hands. It was enough to remind Maryan to pull her hand away. She was blushing as they walked out of the restaurant, tailing Aydin and Hatice.

They took the stairs wrapping the side of the building, the long flight of stone treads coming to an end at the bottom of a narrow residential street.

Under the orange glow of streetlamps, Aydin and Faisal faced off.

The niceties traded at dinner were well behind them by the determination hardening their expressions.

Aydin spoke first. "I'm speaking for my brother as well when I say that we've had our reservations about partnering with your company. I won't lie. I still have my doubts."

No disappointment registered from Faisal.

Suave as ever, he replied, "I thought dinner was going nicely."

"It was very pleasant." Aydin's eyes cast over to Maryan before focusing on Faisal again. "Friendly company makes all the difference."

His wife murmured her assent.

"However, the dinner hasn't settled my...indecision."

"You don't want your company's image besmirched by the indiscreet photos taken of me." Blunt as the end of a hammer, Faisal dealt his blow. Maryan thought it a very brave move. Charge at the problem rather than cower before it. She couldn't say if Aydin would see it the same way, though.

"I'll remind you that your brother was in some of those glossy pictures."

Aydin's eye twitched, his hand palming his beard quickly. "I've spoken to Erkin. He understands my sentiments. We both have businesses to run, and bad press can be very damaging."

"Let's bury the bad press then."

"With a partnership," Aydin hedged.

"Nothing like the good press to offset an unseemly story." Faisal folded his arms after his clever suggestion, his feet spaced evenly apart and his whole stance projecting his steadfastness to this plan for Somalia's dormant gas and oil sector. Best of all, he looked good in his black long-sleeved polo shirt, slim dark-wash jeans and leather spiked high-tops.

As much as she would love to admire him all night, fatigue was sparking from her feet in her wedge sandals and creeping up to weaken her.

The back-and-forth parrying was getting to be too much.

Shuffling her weight, Maryan hugged her arms to protect herself from the coolness riding the twilight. They'd be out there all night if this kept up. Neither man appeared to be budging from his perspective, and they overlooked that they had an audience.

When a shiver raced through her and her teeth clenched from the chill oozing into her bones, Maryan looked to Hatice.

The other woman shared a quick, sympathetic smile. They were in this together, suffering because these two pigheaded men couldn't look past their egos to notice their dates were freezing.

*I'm not Faisal's date!*

No, she wasn't. Which made it worse in a way, as she had no proper reason to be enduring the cold when he'd seemingly forgotten about her.

Maryan heard herself speaking over the isolated sharp throb in her chest, directly over her heart.

"Stop! Please stop."

Both men swiveled their staring to her. Their gazes mirrored identical stupor. As though she'd grown an extra head in the short time that they'd been quibbling over their business dealing.

"Isn't it obvious that you should work together?" She looked between them, doling out her exasperation fairly between them as they both deserved it. "I won't presume to know you, Aydin. However, I've since gotten to know Faisal better this last week. With confidence I can promise you won't find a partner as passionate in a project as him. He's talked nonstop about his hopes for successful drilling offshore Somalia.

"What you probably haven't seen is how his eyes light up when he speaks of helping the families and communities in Somalia, or how he smiles brightly at the positive economic and social changes that could come of a booming oil and gas trade in a developing nation.

"I know money is important to the both of you. You each have people who work for you and who rely on your business expertise and professional decision-making for their livelihoods. But this partnership wouldn't only affect the people nearest to you. It'd brighten the futures of many children and their families.

"Families like my own." Maryan ended her speech with a swift, deep inhale that soaked her lungs with much-needed air. She hadn't meant to talk that long. Hadn't known she held all of that inside until it came spilling out. Like projectile word vomit.

She shook that image out of her head. It was bad enough she was queasy from embarrassment. She didn't need to be picturing it. Shrinking back beside Hatice, Maryan directed her sight down to her wedges and envisioned a massive hole opening beneath her and transporting her far, *far* away.

Far enough not to wonder what Faisal was thinking of her.

Did he hate that she'd stepped onto a soapbox in front of Aydin? What would it mean if he was upset with her? Would she still be welcome in his home?

"She's right," Faisal's voice boomed loudly in the hushed street.

Maryan raised her head slowly, afraid her ears were deceiving her, shocked to find Faisal's smirk matching his bright voice.

"Everything she's said is true. This project is near and dear to my heart. I've…sacrificed time with my daughter for it these past couple of days. I don't want my sacrifice to be in vain. And as confident as I may be in moving forward with my business, a partner for this large undertaking would make my workload easier."

She blinked at his every word, as if she might awaken from a dream.

Surely, he wasn't *praising* her for butting in with her opinion. Possibly humiliating him. *And* destroying any chance he might have had at gaining this partnership.

But as many times as she looked, he was still looking at her fondly.

She returned his smile uncertainly at first, and then bashfully when he winked at her.

"Your family lives in Somalia?" Aydin persisted in wearing his stony expression, his voice emotionless and his hand no longer making sweeping gestures at his beard. "Are they poor?"

"They are," she said hoarsely.

"And do you truly believe the future of a new frontier lies deep in the Indian Ocean near Somalia?"

Time slowed when she glanced at Faisal.

He nodded, his smile benevolent and communicating exactly what she needed to see: his trust in her.

"Yes, I do." She didn't recognize her voice, full of a quiet but powerful self-confidence. It resonated through her and filled the quiet air in the street.

Aydin studied her for an unnerving moment

and then he jerked his head at Faisal, looking to have forgotten her again.

"Erkin and I will have to review a few clauses with you and your team. Does tomorrow morning in your office sound good to you? We can teleconference our legal team in Ankara as well then."

"I'll arrange for it," Faisal agreed.

They shook on the promise of tomorrow before Aydin called to his wife.

Hatice fit perfectly at his side, her demure face glowing now that she was the prize of her husband's attention. Aydin looked different, too, smiling for what had to be the first time that night.

It wasn't long after that when a sleek white town car pulled down the street, looking massively out of place among its mundane surrounds. Limos weren't a part of her world, but Faisal hardly blinked as he raised a hand to bid the couple farewell. As soon as they were gone, he turned for the restaurant.

Pausing once he noticed she wasn't following. "Are you coming?"

She clutched his jacket, swimming in his scent, feeling his warmth mingling with her own body heat. "What happened?"

Faisal's chuckle rubbed her deliciously raw in a way that had a second heartbeat pulsing between her legs.

"You helped secure my partnership deal."

Maryan craned her neck to look back into his eyes, disbelief still rooting her four-inch wedges to the pavement. She saw nothing gleaming down at her but unfiltered awe. It wasn't the world swaying but her body tilting closer to his.

Faisal molded his hand to the curvature of her cheek, his attention hers and hers alone. It jarred her to think they might look like Aydin and Hatice.

The difference being that the other couple were married *and* in love.

Meanwhile, they were nothing more than passing ships. Here together today. Parted forever tomorrow.

Faisal's mouth sealed over her other cheek, his hot breath steaming her flushed skin.

"I'm glad you're here."

He was?

"I wouldn't be if you hadn't asked," she reminded him quietly, still awe-stricken by what happened just now.

"And I'm happy you chose to come." Faisal dropped his hand from her, making her yearn for a second before he held his palm out for her to take once more if she wished it.

And she realized with a startling clarity that she did. More than anything she ever wanted.

She grasped his hand, praying that the night didn't end anytime soon.

\* \* \*

Never had he wanted to kiss a woman as much as he did Maryan.

Faisal ached to taste her again, breathe her hunger in, worship her as she deserved to be worshipped. He slowed as he walked her direction, fresh cups of tea in hand, his eyes riveted on her.

She sat unaware of his longing stare, her head lowered to the phone in her hands, the glow of the screen illuminating her face while an abundance of traditional lanterns brightened the rooftop.

He wasn't holding out for the possibility of another kiss, no matter how much it killed him.

*This is enough.*

Just having her with him for the night. He wouldn't be greedy and beg for more. *Hope* for more.

Absorbed by her, Faisal missed the sharp click of heels behind him. Aslihan materialized by his side.

"I know it's been a long while since we've spoken, yet I can tell when a man is in love."

"I don't know what you mean," he grumbled in Turkish, annoyed and befuddled and embarrassed all at once. *Love?* What did she mean that he was in love?

Aslihan's laughter was shrill and loud.

Loud enough to rouse Maryan's attention from her phone and to them. Her eyes found his immediately, her brows pinching at the center and making him feel as though he'd been caught sneaking one of her delicious Somali beignet-style desserts.

He didn't know why it mattered that he was standing close to Aslihan. Only that it felt wrong. An urge to rush over and explain himself to Maryan barreled into him with its overwhelming power.

"You *love* your nanny."

"She's not *my* nanny." She technically wasn't. Salma had employed her. And in a short matter of days, Maryan would be no one's nanny. She'd be unemployed and free to go wherever she wished to go. Free to do whatever she wished…and with whomever she wished.

Aslihan sniffed. "Fine. If that's the case, you won't mind me asking you to dinner."

"I…can't," he said quickly, softly, his eyes still locked on Maryan.

Aslihan could have prodded him as to why he'd rejected her. Instead, she slipped a business card into his shirt's breast pocket.

"What's that?" he asked.

"It's for the boarding school. Aydin mentioned you were considering the school for your daughter. My father's stepped down as headmaster, but my ex-husband's taken over. We're on good enough speaking terms for me to get you and your daughter an appointment."

Faisal had forgotten he'd been considering this route of schooling for Zara. The past week had been dedicated to sightseeing. With Maryan leaving soon, he'd have to get back to reality eventually.

This was his wake-up call.

"I'll leave you two alone then." Offering a parting smile, Aslihan marched off in her tall, clicking heels, freeing him to uproot his feet and walk toward Maryan.

"You two looked cozy," was Maryan's first words as he grabbed the soft, colorful cushions beside her. The floor seating was meant to encourage comfort and the chance to take memorable photos of the backdrop.

Faisal sensed the change in her instantly. She sat beside him, an aura of suspicion drawing her shoulders up to her ears and fixing her eyes on her phone again.

"She was saying farewell." He placed their teacups aside where they couldn't be knocked down. "And she was also handing me this."

Maryan took the business card from him.

"It's the boarding school I attended. Aslihan's father helped me secure a scholarship to enroll there." The older man had been a family friend of Faisal's parents. "I started late, but I went to the school for the last three years before graduation." Then he'd graduated and gone to one

of Turkey's top universities. Again, on scholarship, but it had been enough for him to know
that he had a chance at securing a well-paying
job with his premier education. Anything to help
his family, especially after his mother's diagno-
sis of depression. What he hadn't expected was
to discover his passion along the way. It happened when he'd secured an internship position
at an investment firm. He had studied and put
to practice what he had learned in school, building a powerhouse network source and a portfolio
of transferable skills. And when he was finally
ready to strike it out on his own, he had done it
with a confidence that paid off, first a million
times over and then a billion more.

"It's in Ankara," said Maryan.

"Would it help if I said that the children have
a week longer for summer and winter holidays?
Also, Zara would have a top-tier education and
a chance to study with peers who could later be
a good network for her."

"She's seven. Networking is the last thing on
her mind."

"I don't know who I'd be without that opportunity." He looked at Maryan, saw her weighing
her thoughts before uttering them.

Then the fight seeped out of her with a soft
sigh. "I know I have very little say on what you
choose to do." She paused, looked into his eyes,

and then gently noted, "Zara won't get to know you from afar. It might seem like the best option for you, given your busy schedule, but ask yourself what it means for her."

He swallowed, promising, "I will." And he meant it, too. He'd consider what she told him. She hadn't steered him wrong with her advice yet.

"Did you call Lalam?" Maryan's moving on was a good sign that he wasn't persona non grata.

"She messaged not too long ago. Zara's asleep, and she's happy to stay longer to watch over her."

"She's an angel." Maryan voiced his sentiment for his housekeeper. "I don't know how you managed to rope her into babysitting last-minute."

He smirked, laughing low. "I gave her a raise."

"You didn't," Maryan said, her tone disbelieving and her laughter sparkling in the night air and rivaling the warmth of the lanterns near them.

"It was the least I could do on short notice. She deserves it, too."

"She does," she agreed with an approving hum.

Grabbing her a cup of tea, he handed it to her. Their silence after was natural, easy, nothing he hastened to disrupt.

"It's getting chillier." Maryan huddled into his coat and shuddered. He'd hoped the tea would warm her up. "Maybe now's a good time to leave."

"Let's take a photo first."

He took their cups again and placed them a safe distance away.

When he turned to her, it was to find Maryan much, *much* closer to him.

It was a repeat of yesterday's scene in his kitchen. With a throat-clearing cough, he pulled out his phone and arranged his arm over the back of the cushions behind her. They were pressed together comfortably, nearly nose to nose, when he glanced over to her. He fell into the deep brown pools of her eyes, her black lashes fluttering lower, her gaze peeking out from under them shyly when she dropped her chin. Behind her the blue-black sky and the city glowing with lights. The shadowy domes and spotlighted minarets of the famed Blue Mosque and its *külliye*—its complex of buildings—hung in the backdrop of their seating. Pigeons that normally haunted the Sultanahmet Square below had retired for the night.

All these observations rushed into his mind, one after the other, until they were a blur because her luscious mouth hovered temptingly closer.

"Are we going to take the picture?"

Nodding dumbly, he held his phone up and touched his cheek to hers, his arm rising from the cushions to fold over her shoulders and curling her into his side where she fit snugly. They snapped low-light photos, their figures illuminated with the aid of his phone's high-resolution front camera and the lanterns sharing the rooftop with them.

He could stay pressed against Maryan like this forever.

For as long as it took to understand what it was that he felt for her.

What had Aslihan called it? *Love.* It couldn't be that.

"Zara will love seeing this photo," she murmured near his ear, her cheek still warming his.

Thinking of his daughter made him think of taking Maryan home. *Home?* Since when had he gotten to thinking of it as her home as well?

"Ready to go?" He lurched to his feet and grasped her hand. Pulling her up against him, their bodies aligning briefly, he thought of kissing her again. Leading her away from their secluded place to the restaurant's exit, he passed Erkin and Aslihan smoking shisha at their table.

Once they were alone again, he hurried to whisk Maryan to his car.

He had no driver today. It'd be just the two of them on their ride home.

*Home.*

The word settled deep in his heart, comfortably, naturally.

He was taking her home.

# CHAPTER EIGHT

FAISAL SET A record driving them home.

Thankfully, he hadn't been stopped for his breakneck speed. The important thing being they were home faster for his risk-taking.

Maryan exited his sports car, not waiting for him to open the door for her this time. She had her sparkly black clutch pressed to the front of her floral see-through bodice. All night she'd tempted him with sneaks of her through the sheer material. It was a miracle he hadn't rushed them back here faster.

"I should head in…" Trailing off with her obvious intent, she glanced at the main home.

He didn't want her to leave him.

It seemed the universe wanted the same thing because his phone chimed with an incoming text. "It's Lalam," he said, skimming the short messages she'd sent, a wide smile lifting his cheeks. "She's asking to spend the night in one of the guest rooms. She's got an exam tomorrow, and it's quicker to catch a ride with my driver to her university."

"That's generous of you," Maryan said, a smile fighting its way onto her rosy cheeks.

"You say generous. I say selfish."

"Selfish?" The smile veered into flirtatious territory with her sultry tone.

Pulling closer into her, he inhaled her spring-time scent. He singled out mouthwatering citruses and fresh notes of herbs, along with her own natural fragrance. Something that was wholly a blend of her shampoo, body wash, and... *her*. Just her.

"I'd be lying if I said I didn't want you to stay with me longer."

Maryan looked away, murmuring, "I wouldn't be opposed to it."

"Will you come up and have a nightcap with me?" A grin fighting its way out. "I have a second stash of baklava upstairs."

Her lips twitched from laughter. "More baklava. You've been holding out."

"No, I haven't. Just waiting for the perfect time to tell you."

"To lure me in, you mean."

"Is it working?" he joked.

"I'll let you know...upstairs." She marched straight for the stairs up to his garage apartment.

Completely enchanted, Faisal followed her and wondered exactly who lured in whom.

Maryan sat enthralled watching Faisal take command of the kitchen.

"Is herbal okay with you? Chamomile?"

"Chamomile's good," she said, blushing when he stared at her a little too long. "Can I help?"

"I've got this." Shrugging his jacket off, he rolled up his shirtsleeves and grabbed a double kettle. She'd seen Lalam use one while making traditional Turkish tea. Faisal caught her staring this time when he flung a smile over his shoulder at her.

"It's called a *çaydanlik*. We use the smaller pot for a stronger brew, and the larger pot for boiled water to dilute the tea." Once he had the kettles on the stovetop, he circled the island to grab the stool by her. "Now we wait."

She'd ask him how long, but the wait time for the tea was the last thing on her mind. She hadn't come up for a nightcap or the sweet promise of baklava.

*I came up for him.*

Maryan allowed that admission to wash over her. Suddenly, a deep fatigue set into her bones. She was drained and done with fighting an unending battle of desire for Faisal. She'd wanted him for more than half this trip. Wanted him more than she had any man. It was a carnal, raw emotion and completely unfamiliar to her. She'd spent all of her life setting aside her wants and needs, for her family. For Hassan. Even for Zara. For everybody else but for herself.

*Enough.* She'd had enough.

Just this once she wanted to do something for herself. She deserved a moment's taste of selfishness.

"So…" Faisal drawled, his smile full of sexy confidence. "I never properly thanked you for accepting my invitation."

"I thought that was what the baklava was for."

He laughed, low and inviting.

Right then, Maryan felt powerful. Unstoppable. She leaned into the delirious power trip and acted in a way she normally would never dare to act. She cupped her cheek and fluttered her lashes lower, teasing, "Okay, then why am I here?"

"Because I didn't want you to leave me just yet."

His seriousness eked a gulp from her.

The atmosphere in the room shifted. It reminded Maryan of the electrified air right before a thunderstorm. You could taste and smell the heavy rains draping the atmosphere, feel it in your soul, know it was coming and be helpless to stop it from downpouring over you.

"What do you want?" She forced the question out into the open.

Judging by the way his eyes widened slightly, she'd shocked him.

"Am I that transparent?" He laughed sheepishly. When she didn't join in, he nervously rubbed his hands down the legs of his jeans and plodded through a response. "I l-like you."

Her heart pulsed. "You like me?"

"I'm attracted to you, yes. Very much. More than I wanted at first, and then I didn't see a reason to fight it."

"Zara," she blurted as though that were a barrier. It should have been. At least it *had* been for her the other night when he'd kissed her, and she'd commended herself for dredging up the strength to stop them. None of that same vigor to fight this was in his apartment with her now.

"I've thought of that. Believe me, it's all I've thought of." He grimaced and then amended, "That's a lie. I have also thought of you. But I said that. Implied it at the very least—"

"One night."

Faisal goggled at her, his jaw falling open.

She'd laugh at his comical reaction, but it would betray the solemnity in the air, and she didn't want to lose momentum on her thoughts. Lose grip of her sudden flare of courage to take what she wanted.

*And I want him. I do.*

"It has to be one night." She had no heart to risk anything more.

"One night," he assented softly.

"Because my family needs me." The explanation bubbled out of her, fear that maybe he wouldn't perceive why she was setting a limit. She'd told him about helping her aunt and uncle. Then there was her dread of leaving Zara behind. She would miss his daughter when she left for California. Picking at that emotional scab by building something real and honest with Faisal was pointless. And she wasn't a glutton for punishment. A boundary of one night would save them both grief in the long run.

"I understand and respect your reasons." His smile was as gentle as his tone, his words sincere and pulsing of his heart.

In that instant, she knew she could trust him unreservedly.

They sat there gazing at each other after, the same breathlessness claiming her seeming to affect him.

Faisal rasped, "I keep thinking about our kiss." He gazed at her mouth, his attention riveted there.

"What about it?" she whispered.

"I want to kiss you again."

She couldn't help the laugh now. "Faisal, we

just agreed to a night. That includes kissing… I hope."

"May I kiss you?" He hadn't lifted his eyes from her lips, his one-track mind adorable and unbelievably sexy when *she* happened to be his singular point of concentration.

"Yes," she gasped.

Faisal pulled in and touched their mouths gently. He stayed still a second before moving, his intimate caress thorough but tender. She parted her lips with a sigh when his hands settled on her thighs, his strong, warm fingers kneading her as they moved higher to her hips. He slid his hands behind her, tugging her deeper into his embrace.

The kettle rattling on the stove ripped him away from her.

"Sorry," he panted, slinging her a weak grin and leaving to give the stove his attention.

She followed him with her eyes, her fingers playing over her tingling lips, her body shining from his kiss.

*One night*, she vowed. *Just this once. One little time won't change anything.*

Why did it feel like that was a lie? Shaking off the odd sensation, she watched him slowly prowl around the kitchen island, his eyes unblinking and resolute in keeping her in his sight.

He grasped her hand, and she marveled at the ache in her core splashing out to all parts of her body. Her breasts grew heavier, her face and neck were warm to the touch, and her legs weren't as steady as they were before she entered his apartment. Before he dropped the mask and looked at her with this unrestrained hunger.

"Kiss me," she implored huskily.

She needn't ask him again. His lips landed on hers and a happy blankness wiped clear her thoughts and other emotions. Everything and everyone but Faisal were pushed out of her mind. She didn't think of her thieving ex, her kindhearted aunt and uncle, her last few days with Zara, her life after her job as the nanny officially ended, her family back home in Somalia. She didn't even think of what came after this, now that it was so clear she'd given a little more of her heart than she intended to Faisal.

Faisal's hot mouth lifted off her and he growled, "I *need* more," and swept her feet out from under her. He carried her to his bedroom and settled her on his bed.

He undressed hastily, his chest bare and all that warm, tensing muscle open to her trailing hands and curiosity. She traced his pebbling dark brown nipples and grew bolder when his breathing puffed out faster.

She tracked her fingertips over his pelvic bones and followed the line of coarse dark hair vanishing beneath his belt.

Faisal caught her hand over the fly of his pants. "Not yet. Let me pleasure you first."

She wasn't going to deny him that.

He claimed her lips again, her mouth pliant to his heavier, hotter techniques. He kissed her masterfully. She didn't think anyone should be allowed to kiss so sinfully. He'd ruin her for other men. Other kisses. Any hope she'd had with someone else puffed out of existence. In a blink of an eye. A stroke of his tongue inside her mouth. He tasted better than flaky baklava or any Turkish delight she'd enjoyed that night. Maybe because she could taste the robust Turkish coffee on his tongue, the sweet lemon of the traditional Turkish confection, and something that was wholly him and made her crave more.

"Kiss me again and again." She moaned the command when he lifted his head to give them both air.

"With pleasure," he growled, taking her lips with his, his body echoing the hungering passion crawling up from deep beneath her the longer he held her in his strong arms.

She laced her fingers at the back of his neck, wrapped her legs around his waist and gasped into their open-mouthed kiss when his hands skimmed her thighs and cupped her backside.

Dark eyes glittering, he broke their lip-lock

and gazed tenderly down at her. "Do you want this?"

"I do." Her heart and head were united in the desire. Still, an insidious hesitance crept over her trust in him. What if he changed his mind and was looking for a way out? And what if he didn't want her as much as she desired him?

As though feeling her doubt, he covered her with his warm, hard-muscled body and kissed her long and deep. Nuzzling her nose with his, he groaned, "There's nothing I want more right now. Nothing I *need* as much as you."

And she believed him.

# CHAPTER NINE

MARYAN SPENT THE next day in a palace. An honest-to-goodness palace—yet all she could think about was Faisal's body atop hers, her nails sinking into his back, his hot lips peppering kisses from her leaping pulse at her throat to her heaving breasts…

What happened last night was a result of a week's worth of pent-up lust. On her part *and* his.

She still couldn't believe he desired her. That she'd made him quake and shudder uncontrollably during their intimate coupling. She'd felt powerful. Like a goddess. But also like a slave to her passion. Faisal the master of her body. And he had given her incomparable sensual bliss. That moment in his arms relieved her of the pressures that'd been weighing on her over the last week and longer.

She hadn't given a thought to anything but rocking and meeting his every thrust.

Embraced the exquisite pleasure he was offering with the whole of her body.

Her limbs continued sparking all through the day. She was a bundle of joyous electricity; her smiles felt infectious, her laughter rolling out easier, her heart as light as air and dancing in her chest. She'd even viewed their private tour of Dolmabahçe Palace in a different light after spending the night with Faisal.

Dolmabahçe's renowned Crystal Staircase shone brighter, and its vast collection of chandeliers gleamed like constellations swinging from gold-framed high ceilings. Luxurious silk, wool and cotton woven Hereke carpets flowed from halls into salons, and hundreds of oil paintings elevated the cultural history of the grand 285-room palace. They'd taken a leisurely tour, stopping and admiring the magnificent architecture and decor, and discovering the history of the six sultans who called the palace their private residence.

She had worried they would get lost when Faisal had them separated from the regular tour group scheduled to go in with them. And when he'd guided them to the closed-off areas of the palace, her paranoia that they'd land in hot water with palace administration and security bounced off him like pebbles.

"I called and asked for a private tour," he'd said, all cheeky smiles. "This way it's just the three of us."

Zara had been delighted. This stop of their

tour was her choice. She'd wanted to see one of the many Ottoman-era palaces in Istanbul. After leaving her behind from yesterday's dinner, it was the least Maryan felt she and Faisal owed his daughter.

That was why she hadn't uttered a complaint when her legs ached from walking the extraordinarily colossal palace from end to end. Faisal had noticed her slowing even when Zara held most of his attention. Without casting focus on Maryan, he'd stop them to rest at convenient intervals. To let *her* recuperate from the long walk.

His kindness resembled his tenderness from their night together.

He had made love to her body gently, slowly, exploring every inch of her trembling, sweat-soaked skin with his hands, his lips and tongue. And after he'd driven their passion wild from the foreplay, they had joined fast, hard and explosively.

She couldn't stop thinking of him in the palace, and her head was still full of the same thoughts as they stepped into the sunlit courtyard.

The palace's cool air-conditioning disappeared. She shivered at the abrupt temperature change and rubbed her bare arms. But it wasn't long before sunshine poured into her the way it flooded the palace courtyard. She dropped her hands from her arms when Faisal's voice called her out of her woolgathering.

"Do you want to grab tea to warm up? There's a café on the other side of the *sarayi*—the palace, I mean." She was getting used to his Turkish slip-ups. Almost as much as she was growing used to his small, kind acts. Soon she'd be an addict to them...

*And his smiles, his laughter, his kisses.*

"I know they have dessert," Faisal said.

Zara's eyes widened with her glee, a bounce in her step as she begged, "Can we please have dessert?"

"It's up to Maryan," said her dad, his eyes twinkling because he knew he had her there.

How could she refuse when Zara pinned her with those puppy-dog eyes?

"Oh, all right." She threw up her hands and laughed when Zara slammed into her for a hug.

She ran a hand over Zara's natural coiling curls, her hair held out of her face with a sparkly purple headband. As her fingers brushed the curls and avoided tangling them, Maryan's heart panged at how she missed Zara's braids. And how she would miss the little girl when they had to part ways.

She had just six more days in this perfect vacation bubble of theirs.

Then she'd have nothing to hold her to Istanbul. Not even one fabulous night with Faisal was enough.

Not unless he…

*Unless he what? Wants me? Actually wants to date me?*

Maryan hated to entertain that train of thought, especially because it sounded as crazy as it had when she'd been lying in his arms, ravished by postcoital bliss. Last night she *had* wanted him to *want* her enough to ask her for more.

To ask her to stay in Istanbul for longer, maybe. Stay and explore what lay beneath their intimate and immediate connection. He hadn't brought it up, though. That left her with a decision of her own. Pining over him and their night of passion, or letting it be what it was: one night with a sexy billionaire.

She still hadn't reached a verdict yet.

"How was your day as a princess?" Faisal nudged her with his elbow playfully, his body heat making her think of their explosive night together.

Zara skipped ahead of them, the lure of dessert before lunch too powerful for her to contain her thrill.

"I think Zara was the real princess. She'd have the sultan's harem wrapped around her little finger." Maryan wagged her pinkie at him and gasped lightly when he caught her hand.

His thumb caressed the soft inside of her wrist, his touch creating that coiling, striking heat in her lower belly. She burned supernova when his mouth hovered over her ear.

"So, is that a 'yes' then? Did you enjoy your day, Maryan?"

She choked through a reply, sputtering, "Not as good as it might have been if I were a sultana."

The joke didn't land as well as it might have had she not trembled under his provocative touch.

Had he not growled back, "I'll make you a queen for another kiss," and made her body grow weak.

They both knew that kissing was impossible for them right then. Public displays of affection in Turkey were not as frowned upon as in other Islamic-dominant countries, but the nation was a study of contrasting histories and opinions. Namely traditional and modern ideologies and lifestyles.

They weren't risking jail time, just jeers from strangers…and queries from Zara. She'd want to know why her dad and nanny were practically embracing.

And if all of those weren't deterrents to toss caution to the wind and kiss Faisal again, Maryan revisited their choice of making this a one-night deal and nothing more. They'd both agreed to it. For the obvious reasons that neither of them seemed ready for a serious relationship. She hadn't needed Faisal to say it; his trust issues were his own and hers were…well, they were her problem.

The fissure of yearning for him shouldn't alter her plan to keep their night what it was: a one-night stand.

The hottest one-night stand ever. Her friends would be pleased that she'd finally cracked and had a rebound after her awful ending with Hassan. So, why did it feel like it was *anything but* with Faisal?

"Zara will see us." She whispered her admonishment. She couldn't bring herself to remind him of their deal from last night.

That appeared to cool him off. Backing away to a safer distance, Faisal tucked his hands in the pockets of his chinos and cast an adorable apologetic look at Maryan. They left it at that, but when they pulled in close again as they entered the café, their hands bumped, and they linked pinkies.

The secret contact was destructive to her willpower against his charm…and yet as deliciously pleasing to her as kissing him.

Faisal suffered when Maryan ordered Turkish delight ice creams for her and Zara.

The waitress delivered the ice creams quickly.

Zara dived in, making a mess of the lower half of her face. She had sticky pink ice cream and pistachios stuck to her chin, but she beamed toothily at him and Maryan, the picture of contentedness.

After helping wipe Zara up, Maryan tasted her ice cream, her mouth closing over her spoon, her eyes widening as she moaned her satisfaction. It was a soft, low moan, appropriate for their setting, but it lanced a bolt of desire through him. He shifted awkwardly in his seat and watched her all the while.

He was torturing himself and couldn't stop.

She licked and sucked her spoon, unaware of his perverted fantasizing.

When his chicken breast pudding arrived, Maryan paused from eating her ice cream and looked at the delicacy on his plate curiously. She stroked her tongue over her bottom lip and drove him to a fantasy of their lips meeting again.

"Want a taste?" He held out his spoon, knowing perfectly well he could have asked the waitress to bring a second spoon.

"What is it, Daddy?" Zara leaned over her ice cream, equally intrigued by his chosen dessert.

"Chicken breast pudding."

Maryan raised her brows. "How is it made?"

"My mom used to make it, and I've watched her do it enough times. You tenderize the chicken until it's soft, then you add milk and sugar, a flavorful thickener like broken rice, and a dash of cinnamon for taste and garnish. It's thick enough for you to shape onto a plate." He gestured to the cinnamon checker design atop the square piece of pudding.

Zara pulled a face and poked out her tongue at the description. "Ew! That doesn't sound very good."

"Zara, we don't say that about food," Maryan chided.

"Sorry, but I don't want any chicken pudding, please." And then as if to avoid any pudding finding its way to her mouth, she shoveled a spoonful of ice cream until her cheeks puffed.

Faisal smothered his laugh with a cough. He didn't want to humor Zara when Maryan was attempting to discipline her.

"So, do you want a bite?"

Maryan eyed his spoon, keeping him on tenterhooks until she nodded. She took his spoon, their fingers touching, his heart beating faster.

She spooned a small bite and tasted the unusual pudding. "It doesn't taste like chicken."

"It's not supposed to. The name is misleading." He accepted his spoon back from her and tasted the dessert, aware that Maryan's luscious lips had been around the spoon crossing his mouth. That naughty thought combined with the delectably sweet and creamy bite of pudding had him stiffer below the belt than he'd been in a long damn time. So long, in fact, he didn't recall ever getting hot and bothered over dessert shared with a beautiful woman.

*Maryan isn't any woman, is she?*

He was starting to believe that more with each passing day. The conundrum being that she had six days left with him and Zara. Six days before she left his world, his life…and any chance at sharing his bed again.

It shouldn't have changed anything. They'd had a perfect understanding last night.

*One night.*

Maryan said it herself, giving him the best out a man like him could want. A man who wasn't in the market for a ring, a white picket fence and all the other trappings that were expected with a vow of forever.

And yet he'd flirted with her *and* tried kissing her outside the café. If she hadn't stopped him, he would have. No questions asked. No doubts. No care as to how it flung a wrench in their plan to seal their passion away in one night.

*So much for my self-control…*

Faisal lingered in the café after they were done to pay their bill and leave a tip.

Maryan had taken Zara outdoors. Zara's giggling was the best music to his ears. Maryan was twirling her. She danced around her nanny, spinning and laughing, and looking so heartwarmingly happy. He dropped enough liras on the table to please the waitress and hurried to join them.

"Where to next?" Maryan asked once he was standing by her.

"I thought we could go check out a park nearby. We'll have to take the car." He'd dismissed his driver again, preferring to chauffeur Maryan and Zara himself. It gave them time alone. Time he cherished more than he had ever thought he would. It was a scary but thrilling feeling.

Like experiencing the heights of their pleasure last night.

Maryan had made him feel *alive*. In a way he hadn't felt when his business plans flowed smoothly. With her in his arms, Faisal felt indomitable. All-powerful. Like he held all the world's good fortune in the palm of his hands. Swept up by that flurry of emotion, he'd had a private thought—what if Maryan *didn't* leave? What if she stayed with him and Zara here in his home, in Istanbul?

He swallowed to no effect, his anxiety floating to the top of the mire of his feelings.

That morning he'd considered asking her to stay longer and not leave them just yet. One look at her blissful expression and his courage evaporated. What if by asking her to stay he ruined the extraordinarily delightful memory they'd just created together? Then he'd have nothing to remember her by.

And it wouldn't be fair of him to ask when she'd been adamant about the limit being one night.

She needed to go home to her aunt and uncle. She'd said it herself. The obligation to her family was greater than his desire to keep her in Istanbul. He had to be selfless, no matter how it pained him to be.

"Are you coming?" Maryan was looking back at him, Zara's hand in hers and a question in her eyes.

He forced a smile for them and nodded his assent.

She gave him a fleeting look of curiosity and then turned to walk away with his daughter toward where he'd parked his car.

Faisal trailed them slower, his head and heart at war over what to do about his growing attachment to Maryan. If he asked her to stay, it'd be a selfish request, but it would also make him happy. But if he let her leave him and Zara he had no doubt in his mind they would lose her forever.

And forever… Forever was the problem.

Maryan had no guess as to what Faisal could be thinking.

They didn't speak while he drove them to their next destination.

He parked his ultra-fancy sports car near the gates of an urban park sharing the grounds of the Topkapı Palace. Another place she'd meant to visit before leaving Istanbul. Before she asked what he was thinking, and whether their plans had changed, Faisal grabbed Zara's hand and stepped up to her.

"We'll go through Gülhane Park and head west first. There's another mosque I'd like to show you."

So far Faisal hadn't disappointed her with his city tour. It helped that Istanbul was new and welcome to her. The city was a paragon of splendid views, friendly citizens, and appetizing foods and drinks.

And Gülhane Park was enchanting.

Wonder-struck, she admired the forested park, its well-tended gardens full of tulips and a tranquil creek. Zara stopped them at a colorful signpost of the park's name to take a photo with her phone, all three of them. Faisal asked a passerby to help them with the picture. While the friendly stranger waited for them to get into position, Zara instructed Maryan and Faisal to sit on either side of her.

"Daddy, you sit here. And Maryan, you sit beside me this way."

Her bossy attitude inspired a laugh from her father and an indulgent smile from Maryan.

The stranger snapped a couple of photos before handing Zara's phone back and leaving.

They took more pictures at Zara's behest in front of the Column of the Goths, an ancient Roman victory column. Once they passed the gate out of the park, Maryan sensed Faisal dropping back to match pace with her. Zara was absorbed with her phone and the photos they'd taken on it and walked ahead of them.

"We should talk." Faisal brushed his hand along hers as they walked closer together.

"About?" she asked.

She had a clue of at least one thing they could discuss, but she wouldn't put words in his mouth. She'd rather hear what he thought without any more suppositions.

"Last night," he said, his voice dropping to a tantalizing whisper. "Being with you was..."

Mind-blowing? Soul-shattering? Exquisitely and incomparably *perfect?*

"Fun."

"Fun?" she repeated, a hollowness setting in all over her body.

He slowed and stopped her with a hand to her elbow. Staring down at her, he frowned, confusion touching his attractive face. "Wrong word?"

"No," she said, forcing herself to say it again when he tilted his head to the side and appeared unconvinced, "*No*, you're right. It *was* fun." *Fun* came out fast and harsh, and with a thread of a growl in the one syllable.

Faisal pulled his fingers through his long curls. She slipped her arm out of his hand and met his troubled eyes.

"You're angry," he said, regret roughening his voice.

"I'm not," she flung back, and walked away.

He caught up quickly, his strides matching her clipped pace. Zara had left them behind when they'd stopped, but she was within visual distance. At least Maryan didn't have to worry about losing her. Clearly the same couldn't be said for Faisal.

*He wasn't yours to begin with. One night was all it was supposed to be.*

She blinked fast to stop the tears. Crying now would unleash all sorts of problems. Faisal would feel guilty and have even more power over her, and Zara would wonder what had gotten her so upset.

*Don't cry. Do not. Cry.*

"Maryan." He beseeched softly and touched her shoulder.

She jerked out of reach, stopped fast and whirled on her heel to finish confronting him. She'd get the last word in, and then they would close the book on this chapter and move on.

But before she said anything, Faisal blurted,

"Fun wasn't the first word that came to mind. It really wasn't."

She sucked her lips in, wanting to believe what he said yet still feeling raw and awfully vulnerable. Keeping silent felt the best course of action. Sure enough, her quiet roused him into continuing his speech or apology or whatever it was.

"Spectacular. Unlike anything I've experienced before. Chemistry off the charts." He shuffled in place then, his palm curling over the nape of his neck and a shyness overtaking him. "For lack of a better word, it was *perfect*. I can't think of any other way to describe it."

"Perfect," she said softly. So softly it was a wonder that he heard her.

"Perfect," he rejoined with a crooked smile. "Are you still mad?"

She shook her head, and his smile spread wider and crinkled his eyes. She turned his words over in her head, her heart lighter and her body shrugging off the frosty remains of her crushed ego and heartache.

They walked then, lapsing into a peaceful silence and following Zara out of the park toward their next stop in that day's leg of the tour.

The New Mosque offered a brief respite from the heated moment in the park.

Pigeons flocked to the square at the foot of the steps into the seventeenth-century imperial mosque. Maryan had done some research on the Ottoman-era structure. It was only one of many mosques constructed by the women closest to the all-powerful sultans of that era. Their wives and mothers.

Faisal purchased three cups of wheat from an elderly merchant working a mobile stall and handed Maryan and Zara one each.

"The pigeons have come to rely on the food," he said, showing Zara how to feed the birds without upending her cup and spilling the wheat inside.

Maryan flicked her wrist, showering wheat grains on the square. A herd of pigeons fluttered nearer to her to scavenge the ground for the fresh wheat. She tossed them more, laughing with Zara when the pigeons brushed their legs in a mad dash to peck the ground clear of food.

When Zara finished her cup, Faisal replenished her with his. He hadn't fed the pigeons, appearing satisfied with watching his daughter experience it for them both.

Eventually he left Zara to continue scattering small handfuls of wheat to the hungry pigeons and wandered over to Maryan.

She sensed he wanted to pick up where they'd left off speaking.

"I am sorry if I made you think anything else,"

he said. "It's just we decided that it would be a night…"

"I know."

"Can you tell I'm regretting it?"

She couldn't believe her ears. Did Faisal want her for *more* than one night? Not that it changed anything. She had a responsibility to help her aunt and uncle. They were family. Family helped each other. She'd been helping hers all her life.

A promise of countless more sultry nights with Faisal wasn't enough to keep her in Istanbul.

And the one thing that possibly could cause her to waver from her plans would never, *ever*, not in a million years happen. It didn't stop her from thinking it.

*If he loved me…*

But, as she knew, *that* was an impossibility.

Faisal pushed his hands into his pockets, gazing at her with an intensity that manifested an ache all through her body. "Am I wrong to assume that we should revisit our terms?"

What would be the point?

Maryan clued in that she'd asked the question aloud when Faisal's eyes grew larger, his brows vaulting higher. *Crud*, she thought, cursing her runaway mouth.

"You're right," he said with a slow nod and the saddest smile. "I shouldn't have even brought it up. No, we were smart to have kept it to one time only. No strings, no commitments and above all else: no complications."

*No hearts broken. No lives irreversibly changed, for better or worse.*

She left those thoughts to herself. It was hard enough recalling why they'd chosen to limit their passionate attraction.

Harder to do it while falling deeper into his eyes and glimpsing the same longing she had for him staring back at her with equal force.

Faisal's ringing phone took that moment to interrupt. Maryan watched him pull it out and stare at it before he looked up to her with an apologetic expression. Figuring it had to do with work, she nodded dismissively before he asked, and he walked away to answer the call.

Maryan went to Zara and found them a spot on the staircase of the mosque to watch the pigeons being fed by passersby.

When Faisal returned to them, he still had the phone in his grasp.

"What's the matter?" Maryan asked, sensing the change in him. There was a pep in his step. A joyous gleam in his eyes. And a curl to his smiling mouth that had her lips pulling up in return.

"It's done. It's really done. Aydin and Erkin have agreed to the deal, and my team's just received their signed preliminary documents." He shook his head, the bewilderment taking hold of his handsome face. "There's still the finalizing of the contracts to complete, but then that's it. We're officially partners."

"And you're building your oil rig and helping Somalia," she added encouragingly.

He looked at her then. *Really* looked at her, his smile softer, his eyes suspiciously glassy. "I couldn't have done it without you."

"What did I do?"

"Aydin was impressed by your speech. I know he was."

"You don't," she argued, losing the battle when his boyish grin dazzled her into silence.

"I just do."

Maryan nudged her chin at his phone and hugged his daughter closer. "Is that what the call was? Do you have to go in to work to oversee your team?"

"No…"

She pursed her lips, not liking that he trailed. Last time he'd done this they'd ended up going to dinner together—

*And having the hottest, most perfect sex of my life after.*

"We've been invited to a party the day after tomorrow to announce the partnership officially."

Before Maryan could give him the third degree, Zara sprang up and hugged her father's legs.

"Do I get to go to the party, too?" she asked sweetly.

Faisal laughed. "Yes, you're coming with us, too." He met Maryan's eyes when he said that last part. She strayed from her doubts, her worry falling off the edge of a cliff, and her memory of their wickedly hot night playing in her mind again. A part of her still couldn't believe their lovemaking meant more to him as well. She never wanted to come down from her cloud nine.

Maryan was riding that emotional high when he said, "I have to make some calls, though, so I'll be a little while. That won't be a problem, right?"

Any red flags that might have been triggered were quashed by her good mood. A mood that Faisal had greatly contributed to.

Which was why she said, "Make your calls. We'll be here waiting for you."

Faisal sneaked a private smile full of heat at her. Planting a kiss atop his daughter's head, he left them then. Maryan watched him go, Zara tucked against her side again, the two of them waiting for Faisal's return. She pushed aside the foreboding sense that she should be worrying. She trusted him. Cared for him.

*Loved him.*

Maryan stiffened and then relaxed into that truth.

She did love Faisal.

She didn't know when it had happened. Probably when she felt perfectly safe in his tender and passionate embrace. Or perhaps it was whenever she watched him with Zara—watched him be playful and loving with his daughter. Then again, now that she gave it her full attention, she must have fallen in love with all of him. And not all at once. *Yes.* That's how it happened. Gradually, as she stripped each layer to the hidden truth of him, down to the most secreted parts, her attraction and attachment to him grew stronger and the love sprung forth naturally.

She loved every side of Faisal she'd witnessed in the past week. Every side of him he'd shown her.

She loved him. Full stop.

# CHAPTER TEN

*BUT WAS LOVE ENOUGH?*

Maryan grappled with that thought more than twenty-four hours later. More than a day since she'd last seen Faisal.

After their trip to the New Mosque, Faisal's phone wouldn't stop ringing. He had barely been present mentally when he'd dropped them off at his home and left for his office. And that was the last time she and Zara had seen him. He had called late last night, right after Zara's bedtime, to ask after her. Maryan had him on the line in hopes that he would want to talk more, but then, citing another boardroom meeting before promising to call her tomorrow morning, he'd hung up faster than she had liked.

He hadn't called but texted her and Zara a short morning message. Apparently "good morning" was his idea of a conversation. He hadn't even responded to her text yet. She'd asked if he was doing all right.

Now several hours later she was entering his

home, shopping bags on both her arms, and a few more in Burak's hands as he shadowed her and Zara indoors.

Lalam took the bags from Burak. Freed of his task, Faisal's security man left with an acknowledging nod.

"Do I take bags upstairs?" Lalam offered.

"Please, thank you," Maryan said, smiling weakly. She wasn't surprised when Zara yawned big. The young girl had woken up earlier than usual to start their busy day. Though none of Zara's earlier enthusiasm was present now. She looked as worn out as Maryan felt.

Noticing that Lalam hovered nearby, appearing as if she had something to say, Maryan regarded her with another fatigued smile. "I'll come up and organize the bags later."

*"Yok,"* said the housekeeper.

From her limited Turkish, she understood that to mean no.

Then Lalam pointed out through one of the glass panes in the front doors. Her finger was directed at Faisal's garage apartment. "Mr. Umar is home."

"He is?" Maryan would've muffled her shock, but it sprang out of her.

"He came home not so long ago."

Maryan thanked her, her mind more alert with this bit of news. Lalam grabbed the bags her hands could carry and headed for the stairs.

"Let's go see your dad."

Zara gripped her hand and they veered out the door, leaving the main home behind and covering the distance to the garage quickly. They climbed the stairs and tried the door. Knocking, Maryan waited with Zara, her thoughts spinning faster the longer it took Faisal to answer his door.

When it opened, he stood there with his earpiece and gestured for them to enter.

She tried not to let her eyes linger where his dress shirt hung open. His fingers made rapid work of buttoning himself up, his hair wet from a shower she presumed, and his woodsy bodywash and aftershave trailing him into the kitchen like a sensual banner. He was pulling out mugs and refilling a kettle. Moving and talking at once, he arranged baklava on a plate and brought it to where they sat on the sofa in his living space.

"It's all set then. Perfect," he said, returning to his call. "I'll have the last few documents delivered in the next hour. Also, send the list of media representatives over to my executive assistant to double-check."

Maryan nibbled on her baklava roll, the flaky dough dissolving on her tongue and bringing her an immeasurable amount of comfort. Watching Faisal work was nerve-racking. Burning the candle at both ends had to be stretching his limits— even billionaires needed a break, didn't they?

And, of course, she had to think of Zara. She deserved to be Faisal's topmost priority. Not his company's stocks, or his shareholders, but his daughter.

*And me?*

No, not her. Most definitely *not her*. She wasn't anyone to Faisal. Pining for him to beg her to stay had consumed her enough. It was starting to feel obsessive.

He finished with his call right as the kettle burbled its signal that tea could be served.

"Zara, you look beautiful," gushed Faisal the second he had their mugs in hand. Once he had the cups safely deposited atop the coffee table, he hugged Zara and held her. "I love your braids and these gold beads."

"Maryan said they would look pretty with my dress," said Zara, her adoration in her eyes when her father pulled back from hugging her and she glanced up at Maryan.

Maryan smiled back down at her. "But Zara chose her own dress, and it's a wonderful choice."

"I can't wait to see it," Faisal praised.

"You will tomorrow, Daddy." Zara yawned then, rubbing her eyes and dropping forward into her father's arms.

"She needs a nap," Maryan told him, their eyes meeting over Zara's head. For a beat they stared at each other silently, and then he broke eye contact and scooped Zara into his arms.

"I'll take her to her room."

"I'll come with you." Faisal stood with Zara, leaving Maryan no other option. Secretly she was pleased that he was putting Zara before his many work-related duties. To think she'd been doubting him. Her concern was unfounded, obviously. She did tell him that he could do it. Be a dad to Zara. Be everything his daughter needed once it was just the two of them.

Overlooking the pain married with that thought, she followed Faisal and Zara back to the main house to do her duty. She was still the nanny, after all.

Only this time it was clear to her, and very quickly, that she was unneeded.

Maryan faded into the background as Faisal carried Zara inside their home and up the stairs to her bedroom. Without having to tell him what to do, he had Zara in the bathroom, running a bath for her, while he rummaged through her dresser for a clean pair of pajamas. Maryan waited outside while he bathed her. Pacing. Worrying, not for Zara but over her unsteady head and heart. They warred with each other. One wanted to tell Faisal of the love for him she'd recently discovered. The other wished to bury any trace of it, smother it with cold dirt and forget it ever flourished to existence.

Which part of her could she trust? Her head warning her from eventual heartbreak, or her heart pulling for love and its restorative magic? The kind of magic bundled in the fairy tales Zara loved to hear.

The bathroom door opened on a flourish of steam. Faisal trotted a sleepy Zara out and to her bed.

She didn't even beg for a bedtime story, snuggling under her bedcovers and falling asleep instantly.

Creeping for the exit together, Maryan came face-to-face in the hall with Faisal.

"Out like a light," he observed, chuckling softly.

"We had a busy day, and an early start."

"I can see that." He studied her, a slow, appreciative sweep over the length of her, his tongue pulling out and dragging over his bottom lip. On anyone else she would have been creeped out. With Faisal, her body grew warmer, and her head jumbled any sense of speech she might have had prepared.

"You and Zara matched."

She ran her hands over her microbraids, the waterfall of long black extensions seamlessly woven into her natural hair and curling softly at the tips. It had taken hours to perfect the look, but she'd been in good hands with Faisal's executive assistant.

"You'll have to thank Rukiya for me. I wouldn't have known what salon to go to here."

"I'll let her know her service was appreciated."

They stood there, on opposite ends of the wide hall, with only the vibrant runner between them…

*It might as well be a chasm with my nerves.*

Maryan pushed her hands into her belly, anything to relieve the pressure of the knots forming inside. She couldn't do this—she wasn't ready to tell him. She'd chosen one night to avoid muddying their situation. And now… Now she wavered between her choices. Should she stay or leave? Should she tell him she loved him, or should she let the distance between Istanbul and Santa Monica erode her love?

She was itching to leap out of her skin, indecisiveness clanging in her brain.

Standing across from him wasn't helping her settle on a decision once and for all.

"I'm going to do yoga while Zara's asleep. I haven't stretched and exercised today." The physical exertion would clear her mind. "I'll be outside if you need me."

"Maryan?"

She paused and spun back to him, her heartbeats so fast she swore she tasted every pulse on her tongue.

"I'm looking forward to seeing your dress, too." Faisal winked and grinned saucily, striding off in the opposite direction, back toward his apartment and office no doubt.

Maryan watched him leave, his flirting giving rise to hope. And that hope eclipsed all her panicked fretting. This whole time she'd thought *she* had to decide. But it struck her that the decision would affect them both. That he had a say, too.

*If he asks me to stay—*

She'd stay. Sort it out with her family but stay in Istanbul with Faisal and Zara.

And if he didn't ask her…

Lucky she was covered there. She had plans for when she landed in California for renovating her aunt and uncle's restaurant, and her job hunting at the community center. This way she'd keep busy with a broken heart.

Faisal attempted working.

But it was pointless. His head was full of Maryan. Something in her eyes earlier had taken hold of his curiosity. She had looked like she wanted to get something off her chest. And it was enough to pull his attention away from the press release announcing his partnership with Aydin and Erkin that his PR team had sent over for his explicit approval. If not that, he had at least a few other tasks on his to-do list for the day, and many more that would need to be completed over the next couple weeks. Not that his busy schedule was anything new.

The distraction from his work *was* a novelty.

He pushed from his chair and paced his office. Then he latched onto the excuse for tea and decided to leave his apartment to head toward the main house for a cup.

The kitchen was eerily quiet. Faisal figured Zara was still sleeping as he'd been gone from the house for an hour. Maryan had told him she'd be doing her yoga. Which meant she would either be in her bedroom…

Or his backyard.

Faisal slowed as he opened his bifold patio doors and passed through the seamless transition into his garden-rich outdoors. His feet had their own agenda, and he was along for the ride.

Walking out into his carefully architected oasis never failed to calm him.

Several large pots housed palm trees, their recognizable fronds swaying to the warm winds that passed through the garden. A plethora of colorful, vibrant tropical flora encircled the garden and its water features. A two-tier fountain was the focal point. The fountain's bowls were held up by a pride of three lions, their gaping maws and sharp teeth lifelike and a testament to the sculptor's skill. Further in the recesses of the garden, the rippling shallow waters of a man-made pond was at the foot of a crafted waterfall. The trickling water from both fountain and pond completed the tranquil mood of the cultivated garden. Most thrilling of all, the full-foliage shade of two massive oak trees lent a privacy to the space and separated his vast manicured lawn from his garden paradise.

Normally, escaping to his terrace was a joy in and of itself.

Only it was tenfold more gratifying now that Maryan was in his backyard.

She was under the gazebo and in the middle of a complicated yoga position that had her hands and arms supporting her lower half. She had her back to him and had no clue when he stood a foot from where she exercised, blissfully clueless to her audience of one.

*Her very mesmerized audience of one.*

He wiped his mouth, fearing drool.

She lowered to the yoga mat and stretched her arms up before transitioning gracefully into her next position. Before she raised her taut rear up again and he lost his train of thought forever, Faisal coughed loudly, sputtering from the force. He coughed for real, tears pinching the corners of his eyes, while Maryan dropped to the mat and whipped her head around to him. Shock morphed to concern on her lovely face.

"Are you okay?" She reached for her water bottle on the gazebo bench, looking prepared to offer him a sip.

"Just a tickle in my throat," he croaked with a blush he could feel warming his face.

Maryan didn't argue, letting it go and saving him from fumbling through more of his embarrassment.

"Is Zara awake?"

"I don't think so." His daughter was a bundle of energy, as most kids her age were. She'd have been downstairs, tearing the house apart, if she were awake. He was confident in this. "I came for tea."

"What happened to your stash in the apartment?"

He rubbed his stubble-heavy jaw, a chuckle rolling out of him. "Okay, you got me. I had a need for company. Nothing makes tea sweeter than enjoying it with someone else—or so my parents say."

"I wouldn't mind a cup of herbal."

"Would you settle for green? I hear it's good… er…post-workout." This was the part where he didn't allow his eyes to trace down her wrap sweatshirt—envisioning her body under the drapey top. Or to her scrunched leggings that accentuated her round backside and thighs and reminded him of the strength he felt in her legs when they'd been wrapped around his waist.

*And now I know where she's getting that strength.*

"I'll grab the tea for us," he said, desperately needing the time-out to get his head on straight.

He'd come to her for a reason.

It was only as he was pouring their green tea into their cups did Faisal understand what that reason was.

*I want her to stay.*

More than he wanted to give in to his fear that she'd turn out to be like one of the many money-hungry dates he'd had in the past. Taking his heart out of the equation had done wonders for his peace, even as it reinforced the idea that he'd never find love. Not with his wealth luring in the wrong kind of women.

And Maryan didn't feel wrong. She felt crazily, miraculously *right*.

That was why he had to speak up. Say something. Give voice to the wild but wanted emotions she'd inspired in him.

He carried their cups on saucers back to the garden, an eagerness to get back to her in his hurried steps.

"...perfect dress! It cost a lot, but Faisal's generous. You'd like him, Habo."

*Habo.* She was talking to her *aunt*.

Faisal stepped behind the giant potted palms before the gazebo. Under their cover, he listened at the cost of his breaking heart.

"My hair is beautiful, too. I'll take a picture for you at the party, show you all the fun times I'm having."

Was that what he was to her: *just* fun times?

His shoulders slumped, his grasp on the saucers tightening, the cups jangling louder when he backed up at her nearing voice. He miscalculated one step. The next few seconds happened fast. With a startled grunt, he fell back, the hot tea flying and dumping onto his lap and the front of his dress shirt.

Maryan turned the corner, phone pressed to her ear and with eyes as large as a full moon. Faisal imagined he looked a sight. The teacups and saucers scattered on the lawn, his shirt and pants drenched at the front, and his pain and misery finding company in his humiliation.

"I'll call you back, Habo." She hung up and rushed to him, quick on her feet, her hands gripping one of his arms and helping him from the ground. "What happened?"

"Lost my footing," he grumbled, hating that he already sounded as miserable as he felt.

She looked to where his shirt stuck to his chest, a wrinkle in her brow. "Does it burn?"

"I'll be fine. Only my ego's hurt," he lied.

Cowardice had him stooping to pick up the cups and saucers, a chip in one teacup eliciting a groan—Lalam wouldn't be happy. She prided herself on preserving his tableware. Cleaning up kept him busy for a minute or two, and then he had to meet Maryan's eyes again.

She was worrying her bottom lip with her teeth.

Did she know that he'd overheard her? He hadn't meant to eavesdrop. But it was what it was. Still, he didn't want to do this now if he could avoid it.

Before he could wrestle with his choices on what to do, Maryan got ahead of him with whatever was clearly bothering her.

"I was talking to my aunt."

"Oh?" He aimed for nonchalant, testing the waters with what she knew and what she didn't.

"She's been calling me, and I hadn't had the time to call back last night."

"I bet she misses you."

"Well, I miss her, too." Maryan chewed her lip again, her brows slashing lower.

Faisal hardened his jaw, refusing to give in to the instinct to make her worries go away. "Two weeks is a long time. I suppose you're happy it's coming to an end?"

She frowned. "I'll miss Zara."

*What about me?* he wanted to ask petulantly.

"My aunt was confirming my flight time again. My uncle wants to pick me up at the airport."

He swore a thread of hesitation skirted her voice at the end. Not that it softened the blow of her words. And they were like a punch to his juddering heart.

*This was it. She's leaving.*

And he had to let her go. He promised he wouldn't hold her down past one night. She'd bared her heart to him in a short time, trusting that he'd understand—and *he did*, but it didn't change the fact that he burned achingly to beg her to stay. But the plea dried up on his tongue.

It would be cruel to ask her. She'd told him how her parents had planned for her to make a life in America alone. Then how her ex-boyfriend abused her confidence. Robbing her of this decision to stay or leave would be betraying everything they'd shared.

The only thing that might solder her by his side was the very thing he'd avoided thinking too hard on. *Love.* Faisal let it breach his mind, but all he could think was how very wrong it would be to use the power of deep affection on her. Not when he wasn't certain of it, and when he didn't know if love would be an unquestionable fact.

"It's always nice to see family at the airport." He spoke slowly and over the rushing blood in his ears.

His chest stung where the tea was cooling on his clothes, and his backside ached from his hard fall. A strange bitterness filled his mouth, and a sweetness tainted the air he breathed—it was either Maryan's fragrance or the garden. In the end he settled on it being a little bit of both, her scent and the greenery circling them. But soon her scent would be gone from the space.

Too soon she'd be gone.

"It'll be good to see them again," she said softly, tacking on, "Though I mean it. I'll miss Istanbul. Even the parts I haven't seen yet."

Those words should have been a remedy reversing his unhappiness. But all he processed was her tense, fake smile. There was something she was holding back from saying. Did it have to do with what she'd been saying to her aunt? What did Maryan tell her about him?

He stopped his overactive mind from churning out conspiratorial theories, all centered on his immense personal wealth.

*She isn't like that.*

He just knew she wasn't after him for his money. Even so, she couldn't want him. He was a bundle of trust issues. And she had explained why love wasn't for her. Knowing this and then subjecting her to his mistrust would be cruel.

*It's me. I'm the problem.*

Faisal stood taller at that unnerving revelation.

Because it was, no matter how he looked at it. He wanted her to stay, but he wasn't willing to lower his defenses and let her in. And if by some chance they did last forever, it would be a forever spent with him always on guard—always doubting—always vigilant for the first sign she'd unravel his heart.

"Faisal?" Maryan's voice wrenched him out of his thoughts.

"We still have some time to squeeze in a few more landmarks." He smiled forcibly, rattled by his self-reflection. "Unless…you'd like to stay on as Zara's nanny?"

He knew the tasteless joke wouldn't land. He bargained on it. There was too much between them now, and the sex had been both a blessing and a curse. A blessing because he'd found someone he genuinely liked, and a curse as he couldn't in good conscience have her work for him and pretend that she meant nothing to him.

She'd never be just the nanny to him.

*Because she never was.*

Maryan's face fell.

"We both know I couldn't."

"Maryan, I was kidding…"

She hummed as though she believed him, her tight-lipped smile filling the pained silence that followed.

"I should go in, get changed, showered, check

on Zara." She listed her excuses, her feet moving for the patio doors.

Faisal heard himself mutter, "Of course," his head lowered, shame keeping him from looking her right in the eye.

This was best for them. He couldn't hold her down with a false promise of feelings he was still sorting through. Maryan deserved a clear answer, and he didn't have it for her right then.

He didn't know if he ever would.


Maryan didn't stop until she reached her bedroom.

She headed out onto the balcony, the air fresher outside, her lungs no longer ready to burst from lack of sufficient breathing. Faisal had made her breathless—again. But in a way that also made her feel like the smallest, most insignificant being in the whole world. She wanted to cry. And cry. And never bother reaching out and grabbing what she wanted most, no matter how promisingly close and deceptively hers it felt.

*He wasn't ever mine.*

Accepting that with a torturous swallow, she let free the first sob of many.

She cried quietly, curling down to a crouch and squeezing the stone balusters for support. Waking Zara next door wouldn't help, and alarming Lalam would bring forth questions Maryan wasn't ready to answer.

The tears felt endless. She let them out with soft hitched breaths. Crying because she *wanted* to stay. Maryan understood that clearly now. She had made her decision, and then she'd prayed that Faisal would show her some sign that he felt the same about her departure. That he wanted to see just how far this electric attraction between them could go.

But…she should have known it was too good to be true.

She'd just told her aunt about him. And although she hadn't mentioned any romance, her Aunt Nafisa had teased her anyway. The warmth and hope she had felt earlier was gone.

Why hadn't he asked her to stay? They had grown close over a short span of time. Faisal had listened to her. They'd talked. Shared their hurts and fears, and then connected on a physical level that outshone her previous relationships. The only thing that seemed off the table from the start was a possibility of forever.

But she still stupidly hoped.

And now her heart was broken.

And…and…she wiped under her stinging eyes and brushed her hot cheeks, a rush of anger overtaking her. She had four more days. None of them *had* to be spent in Faisal's home. Seeing him every day would be a special kind of torture for her. And she wasn't a masochist. Maryan did think of Zara, and her anger cooled slightly, a sorrow filling the spaces it left vacant. If given the option, she'd have wanted to keep Zara close to her forever. She loved Faisal's daughter. No distance would change that for her. Not ever.

Packing her suitcase was something she'd known she had to do eventually. Even when she had deigned to be silly and hope to stay, a part of her had resigned herself to this being a possibility. She placed the last few items in, closed the lid on her luggage and rolled it by the door, before going in search of Lalam. On the way, she stopped by Zara's room, her feet unbudging. She touched the door with a trembling hand, her eyes filling up again, and her heart tugging down, down, deep down into her stomach.

Pressing a kiss to her palm, she touched the door one last time and left in search of Faisal's housekeeper.

Lalam's voice drifted from a slightly ajar bedroom door.

Faisal was in there, too. Maryan slowed at the sound of his deeper voice. Nothing he said was discernible, though, so he must have been farther in the room. Too far for her to eavesdrop.

She waited nearby for Lalam, and not for long. "Miss Maryan? Is something wrong?" The amiable housekeeper caught sight of her only after she closed the bedroom door behind her.

She glanced down at the first aid kit in Lalam's hands, recalling Faisal burning himself in the garden. *Is he hurt badly?* she wanted to ask, but bit the inside of her cheek. She'd see for herself when she spoke to him.

"Nothing's wrong," she fibbed, offering what she hoped was a reassuring smile before pointing to Faisal's closed bedroom door. "Do you think he'd mind if I knocked? I need to speak with him."

Lalam gave her an encouraging nod before walking off, seeming none the wiser of the turmoil in Maryan's heart.

"Come in." His voice was muffled but loud enough to answer her rapping knuckles.

Faisal was stepping out of a massive walk-in closet opposite his king-size bed. He tossed the tea-stained dress shirt in his laundry hamper when she walked in. He slowed and stopped, staring at her. The curtains were drawn to his room, the natural light showing her the glamour of his master bedroom *and* the clear alarm in his widening eyes.

He dropped his gaze suddenly, fixing it on the carpeted floor. "Hey. I thought you were Lalam."

"I saw the first aid kit. Are you hurt badly?" The question blurted out of her. Funny how even after he'd knocked her heart into despair, she was concerned for him. She blamed love. Stupid, silly, maddening love.

"The burns sting a little, but I was just about to take pain reliever for it."

The fact that he kept his eyes glued to the carpet spoke the kind of volumes that made her eyes water again. Maryan blinked furiously, glancing up at the ceiling with its pretty pendant lighting and willing the watery heat from making an appearance. She didn't want to cry in front of him. She wasn't certain how he'd react, not after he hadn't made any move to ask her to stay. She couldn't be sure of anything between them anymore.

"I'm leaving," she said, glad her voice was strong, crisp, full of the certitude she hadn't felt a moment ago.

That snapped his head to her. *Finally.*

"As grateful as I am to have been able to be close to Zara in your home, I've overstayed my welcome."

"Maryan, you don't have to go yet."

But she had to go eventually, so did it matter when she walked away?

"If it's not a bother to you, I'll wait until Zara wakes up. I want...*need* to tell her myself." She knew what it felt like when adults made decisions for children and expected them to follow along. She wouldn't leave like a thief in the night and shatter any trust Zara had in her. "Then I'll book a hotel and grab a taxi."

Faisal scowled. "No way. If you're intent on leaving, my driver will take you where you please."

She could've argued, but then they would be standing here longer, and she couldn't fight to hold back the brunt of her emotions. The tearful anger, the disheartenment, and above all, the disappointment. In him. In herself.

"Do you have to go…now?" he pleaded.

She wasn't so naive anymore to read more into his plea. It was on Zara's behalf that he was persisting on changing her mind. He'd made it loud and clear that none of this begging was him wanting her.

"Sorry. I should respect your wishes," he apologized quickly.

*But it isn't my wish! I want to stay here, with Zara. With you!*

She clamped her teeth over her bottom lip to stop from shouting the words out into the open.

Faisal's pinched brows, downturned mouth and hard jawline—all of it registered to Maryan as his way of building a wall between them. It gave her more of a reason to walk away while they were still being civil. Instead, she waited, expected him to address the elephant in his expansive bedroom, and then opted to do it herself.

"Also, I won't be attending the party."

"This is because of me," he said in a low, rasping voice. "Zara will hate that you won't be there."

She wouldn't be guilted into going, and he must have realized that because he apologized a second time.

"I'm sorry. I don't know what's wrong with me." He sucked in a whistling breath and scrubbed a hand down his long face. She wasn't sure why *he* looked so unhappy. Wasn't her leaving what he wanted?

Faisal sighed then, interrupting her quiet bafflement as he continued.

"This is my fault. I'd expect nothing less. I just wanted you to be comfortable here, with us. Obviously, I haven't been the best host in the past hour or so." He smiled weakly. "Thanks for staying to explain to Zara. She'll take it better hearing it from you."

Maryan had thought she'd feel gratified at hearing his misery. Far from it, she battled her weakening determination as she left his room to hide out in hers again. She wanted to feel like this was how it should be. He hadn't asked her to stay longer. He'd made her feel miserable. It should have felt good to see him just as downcast.

Newsflash: it didn't.

Worse, she was rethinking whether this was the right choice for them after all…

# CHAPTER ELEVEN

SOMEHOW, HE'D SURVIVED the events of yesterday.

Maryan left for her hotel after she spoke to Zara, and with a terse farewell to him, abandoning them to experience their first night without her.

And what a night it was. He hadn't slept long enough to dream. After a tousle with his sheets and some fitful rest, he awoke for an early start to his day. He was only beginning to feel the sleep deficit now. Faisal rubbed his tired, aching eyes, a toe-curling yawn taking him by surprise. But not nearly as surprising as a call from his mother, first thing in the morning. He blinked at the missed notification on his phone, puzzling as to what her call could be, and then panicking as his imagination spun the worst-case scenarios as to why she'd phoned him outside her regular hours.

"Mom? Are you all right?" He stopped himself from asking if her new treatments were not helping with her depressive moods.

She quickly assured him of her good health, and then she heaved a put-upon sigh. "Why is it that my son does not call me when good news has happened for his company? Why is your sister the one to tell your father and me first?"

With everything that happened, his memory had lapsed in informing his family. But the news would have circulated online and reached his sister. He knew she liked to keep tabs on him whenever she wasn't actively interrogating him about his life.

Still, the thought of his bossy little sister teased a smile from him. "How is Yasmin?"

"She wants to see her niece." His mom tsked good-naturedly. "And your father and I want to see our sweet-faced Zara, too."

"I promise you'll see her soon. Actually, I'm hoping we can visit sometime next week." He had it all set up, but his planning had fallen by the wayside when Maryan arrived. And then again when she checked out of his home early to finish up her final few days in Istanbul in a hotel. Just like she would have if he hadn't interceded and talked her into staying with him and Zara.

His mother didn't know that, though, so he couldn't unload his troubles onto her.

Perceptive as always, his mother stated, "You sound like you are very busy."

"I am, but never for your calls. You know that."

For his family, he'd drop everything. They were all he had. All he could trust.

*Especially now that I pushed Maryan from me.*

"Are you eating well? Do I have to come for a visit and make you all your favorite foods?"

God, would he love that.

"Zara's nanny made *kac kac*. It tasted like yours." The highest praise from him. Maryan had given him a taste of his childhood.

"She can cook?" His mother harrumphed. "And you let her go?"

Faisal let out a belly laugh, but the tears in his eyes were not solely attributed to his mirth. There was a despondency left after the laughter stopped. It ate away at any remaining joy until he had to fear that nothing would be left soon.

"I warned her about your matchmaking."

"You should have brought her with you, that's what you should have done."

His mother's teasing was a healing salve to the wounds afflicting his soul. *Self-inflicted*, Faisal noted sternly. He could've kept her with him. Or tried to. Instead, he'd thought he was doing the right thing by letting her go.

"I will have to test her *kac kac* myself."

"She's gone," Faisal said gruffly, short with himself and forgetting who he was talking to.

His mother latched onto this with silence first, and then a soft, "This is what's upsetting you," nailing him to the wall with a truth he'd preferred to have dusted under his office rug.

"Mom…"

"No," she spoke with a sharpness that stilled his tongue, "you like this nanny."

"Her name's Maryan…and, yes, I do. *Did.*" He huffed, "It doesn't matter. She would have left at the end of her two-week stay."

"Love doesn't have a measure of time," exclaimed his mother, her exasperation clear as a bell.

There it was again. She'd be the second person to call him out on loving Maryan.

"I didn't say I *loved* her." He grunted when he bit his tongue, his confusion about his feelings physically harming him now. Guess it was what he deserved after the way he treated Maryan in the end. She'd done so much for him. She could be humble all she wanted, but she'd instilled a confidence in him with Zara, she had believed in his dreams for Somalia, and then she had stuck up for him in front of Aydin. All of that on top of the body-melting pleasure she'd given him in bed.

No one had to tell him he was a fool to let her walk away.

"I did not raise an idiot for a son."

"Hooyo…" he began affectionately, snapping his mouth closed when it didn't work and she tsked louder.

"You love her, and you have made a big mistake when you let her leave."

"She wanted to leave, Mom. I wasn't going to lock her in her room." He stopped breathing as soon as the words tumbled from his mouth. He didn't even argue this time on whether what he felt for Maryan was love or not.

"She was staying with you?" His mother's incredulity had him drawing the phone from his ear and face-palming. He pulled his face out of his hands when she finished lecturing him about the impropriety. And he only knew it was safe to place his ear back on the receiver when a silence dawned on her end.

"Mom?"

"Do you love her?" she asked gently and with none of her chagrin at his indecorum.

Without thinking, Faisal avowed, "I...think I might."

"It is never an easy thing to undo our faults. Much easier to make a mistake than repair one."

"I don't know if I *can* fix this."

She was quiet long enough for him to worry that the line had cut off. But then his mother said, "You will. My son may be an idiot—he's also zealous for the things he loves most."

Faisal brushed the back of his hand over a cheek, coming away with a wetness that matched the love he was feeling from his mother. And not just her. He had a chance to speak to his father, and then his sister, both in congratulatory moods over the news of his lucrative partnership. After he bade them farewell, he rubbed his chest above his heart and relished the tremendous weight that vanished sometime during the call to his family. Their support was all he ever relied on. Their love strong enough to banish the negativity that had been weighing him down.

And keeping him from realizing that his mom's advice aligned with his heart's deepest truth in that moment.

*I love Maryan.*

He saw that so clearly now and wanted to thump his head over his desk at the obviousness. Everything he'd been feeling. All the confusion surrounding his emotions when he was near her, the clawing worry of what she thought of him, the heartache at her departure, and the surety that *nothing* would feel right for him without her. Each was a sign that he loved her.

But she had no idea of how he felt about her truly, and he'd have to remedy that first.

# CHAPTER TWELVE

MARYAN THOUGHT SHE'D settled the matter of the party.

But she was exiting Faisal's luxury sports car, lifting the voluminous, tiered skirt of her crystal-and-tulle designer ball gown, and climbing the endless stone steps to the opulent mansion at the top. Behind her Burak shadowed her dutifully. He'd come bearing the handwritten note from his boss, along with the expensive dress in its dress bag. She had left the gown behind when she fled Faisal's home for a hotel.

*I might be the last person you want to see, but I would love if you could attend the party tonight.*

Faisal had been right about her not wanting to see him. At least that was how she felt when the note and dress arrived at her hotel suite by way of his security. Then as the day passed, and she reread his message, she sensed a shifting in her heart. It wasn't as stony and unimpressed by Faisal's quiet plea.

Then her curiosity ran away with her.

Had he changed his mind possibly? Did he, in fact, not want her to leave Istanbul? And if so, why?

She was resolute that she wouldn't be a booty call to him. Fantastic as it was, sex alone wasn't fulfilling for her. She wasn't in the market to be an au pair, either. As much as she loved Zara, being her nanny with Faisal as her boss was a recipe for disaster. She'd abandoned one unhealthy relationship, and she wasn't trading her ex-boyfriend for fast, fun times with Faisal.

*I'm not asking for a proposal, either.*

She wasn't ready for that leap of faith. Marriage was serious business. When she imagined her wedding day, it was opposite the man she loved and felt confident was her soul mate. She didn't know if Faisal could be that—and she realized she wouldn't ever know because she hadn't *told* him she loved him.

That was why she'd come to his party.

She needed to get her truth off her chest, once and for all. He had to know.

*It doesn't matter if he feels the same.*

All her life she'd learned to not question the people she cared about and who supposedly cared for her. She had done it with her parents when they'd packed a small suitcase for her one-way trip to America. She hadn't loved her ex-boyfriend, but she'd trusted him, and she hadn't thought to question that bond of trust.

They had made their decisions. Left her with the mess. And now—

*Now* Maryan had a chance to speak up where Faisal was concerned. And if he didn't reciprocate her love, then at least she'd get to see Zara in person one last time…

"Is he inside?" she asked Burak, looking back to find him waiting on her. For once he had his sunglasses off. Possibly as the sun had long set, and it wouldn't make sense to wear shades right then. But with nothing obscuring his eyes, Maryan could see him squinting through a study of her. He almost looked as though he had something to tell her. "What is it?" she wondered.

"It's not my place to say anything, but he's not been himself today."

"Pardon?" She could tell herself whatever she wanted, but her heart wasn't beating loud enough to drown out Burak's observation.

Not elucidating on what he informed her, he simply said, "Yes, he's inside, waiting for you."

With a look down at the line of luxury vehicles snaking up to the front of the waterside mansion, their headlights shining brighter alongside the Bosporus's dark, still waters, she fortified herself for what awaited inside the shining windows of the mansion.

*And who*, she thought with a nervous gulp.

\* \* \*

"A toast, to our partnership. May it see us weather the challenges and celebrate the victories ahead."

A chorus of clinking glasses spread through the spacious salon from the dais in the center. Faisal raised his glass of raki after his speech, first to his new business partners, Aydin and Erkin, and then to their guests, including a curated group of media representatives. This was one piece of news they wouldn't doctor into a scandal of his personal affairs.

Stepping down from the dais, he smiled wide and laughed on cue, working the room as he was expected before he found refuge in the corner where Zara waited with Rukiya. Nodding his thanks to his executive assistant, he abandoned his untouched drink and lifted Zara into his arms and spun with her in place, thrilling in her laughter.

"May I have this dance, little princess?"

She bobbed her head, but the luminous silver flower crown threaded to her braids didn't budge.

It was as Maryan said. Faisal thought Zara adorable in her cap-sleeve dress and strappy party shoes. He set her down and showed her how to balance on the ends of his feet, not caring if her shoes scuffed his. Then he duck-walked, turning circles carefully to the music and creating their own beat when the couples around them swayed to a different melody. When the band switched to a lively folk song, Faisal popped Zara off his feet and he twirled her around and around, her glee casting out the darkness glooming his mind, but also forcing him to face what he'd lost.

He didn't mean to think of her, but it was hard not to see Maryan in every part of his life now.

At his home, at work—when he couldn't stop from thinking about her—and now, here, at this party that she refused to come to, while he was dancing with his daughter and crafting another amazing memory.

He'd sent her a note and had Burak deliver it. *But it wasn't enough*, he surmised bitterly.

None of the bitterness targeted at Maryan. This was on him. And now he had to nurse his hurt and disappointment alone.

"Daddy?" Zara tugged his hands to get his attention. Once she had it, she gestured for him to crouch. Then when he did that, she hugged him, her small arms squeezing around his shoulders and prompting him to embrace her just as tightly.

"What was that for?"

She touched her hands to his clean-shaven face, looking as solemn as an energetic seven-year-old could. "You look sad, Daddy."

"Do I?"

He hated that it was obvious even to her.

"Are you sad because of Maryan?"

They'd discussed her nanny's departure, and Faisal comforted Zara as best as he was able. Finding that he wasn't half bad at it without Maryan to guide him.

"It's okay to be sad. I miss her, too."

"I know you do, sweetheart," Faisal murmured, kissing her forehead. "I also know that she misses and loves you very much."

"Can I talk to her tonight?"

"Remember what she told you? She said you can call her whenever you like." It was exactly what he expected from her. Maryan had to be grieving the change of not seeing Zara every day as well. And he'd caused their pain, unnecessarily so. All he had to do was tell Maryan how he felt. Tell her that he loved her, and though marriage was far from his mind still, he had a strong feeling that with time it could be in their future.

Not that it mattered now. That ship had long sailed. Her flight home three days away. And she hadn't spoken to him when she'd called Zara earlier today. Besides a short text letting him know she'd arrived at the hotel safely, she hadn't reached out to him at all.

The worst part being she didn't respond to his note.

Since leaving to deliver the note an hour ago, Burak hadn't reported anything, leaving Faisal with the understanding that he'd have to learn to live without Maryan because she wasn't willing to forgive. Regardless of his efforts to make his grand declaration of love and try to sweep her off her feet.

"Daddy, don't be sad. I'll love you for both me and Maryan."

Zara's proclamation earned her another bear hug from him. At the end of it, his daughter wriggled free and grinned, asking, "Can we spin again?"

He spun her a few more times before swinging her up into his arms and swaying with her in his embrace.

"Maryan!" It wasn't so much Zara squealing in his ears or her bouncing in his arms that stopped Faisal. It was what she said and who she called to.

Sure enough, when he turned his head to where Zara smiled, he spotted her nanny walking past. Maryan seemed not to have heard Zara over the din of the party, her back to them as she retreated deeper into the mansion. These old Ottoman-era waterside houses were sprawling and mazelike. Throw in a guest list of nearly two hundred people and the sinking dread of losing her was in the realm of possibility.

Setting Zara on her feet, he walked her back to Rukiya.

Burak was there, too.

"Is she here?" Faisal knew what his friend's answer would be, but he was further reassured that he wasn't imagining Maryan when Burak nodded.

"She wanted to explore the house."

Of course she did. It sounded just like her.

Leaving Zara to their care, Faisal went to search for her. Having Maryan so close, knowing that she had come after all, was the kick in the pants that he needed to see his mission through. By the end of the night she'd know that he had fallen in love with her, and if she deigned to have him, he would seriously attempt to be the man she desired. A man who was worthy of her, body, heart and spirit.

Scouring the house for a sign of her was more of a challenge than he had prepared for.

People crowded every room and corner. Erkin had overseen the guest list, and with Aslihan, they had seemingly invited the whole of Istanbul's elite. Faisal encountered politicians to pop stars, and even an actor or two from one of his favorite Turkish dramas. Stopping to chat wasn't an option for him right then, no matter how much the idea of an autograph was appealing. Finding Maryan was his single-minded pursuit. She wasn't in any of the lavish salons, their gilded ornamental walls and theatrical furnishings lovely, but nowhere close to being lovelier than her face.

The rooftop terrace shone with countless string lights, but their radiance was dimmed without the presence of Maryan. He even tried the Turkish hammam with no luck. The resplendent architecture of the bathing rooms standing empty.

Naturally, as his search area dwindled, his concern of having lost her again began to set in. By the end of his tireless searching, he walked slower, dejection slumping his shoulders. That was it. He'd looked high and low, *literally*. Maryan wasn't in the splendid waterfront Turkish manor hosting his party.

Faisal brushed a hand over his head, remembered he'd had his curly hair shaved for a cleaner, professional look, and groaned loud, his frustration echoing off the darkened walls of the lonely room he'd ended his search in. He couldn't even indulge in tugging at his hair. Missing his curls, and missing Maryan even more, he gazed mindlessly out the floor-to-ceiling windows wrapping the far side of the room. The view was of the front of the house, the obsidian strip of the Bosporus separating the row of Empire-style waterfront properties from the rest of Istanbul on the opposite side of the strait's waters.

No natural lighting gleamed off the ink-like surface of the waterway. Instead, it reflected the lights from the mansion's many narrow windows

and the lampposts irradiating the private port…
and Maryan.

Faisal did a double take, but she didn't vanish
from where she paced alongside the Bosporus
down below.

He pulled himself away, realizing that he had
to seize this opportunity while fate was so gener-
ously offering it. Getting down to her was another
obstacle to surmount. It took a while to cross the
more crowded areas of the mansion before he
strode out a back door and into the night. Then
it was all about how fast he could jog to where
he'd seen her last.

It felt like an age had passed when he halted
a few feet from her, her back to him again, his
heartbeats pounding in his ears from a combina-
tion of his jogging to her and from the exuberance that he hadn't lost her.

*Not yet.*

A series of vibrations from his phone hummed
in his inner coat pocket. Faisal halted his movement forward just as Maryan whipped around
to face him. Her eyes rounder than ever before,
one hand clutching her phone and the other her
sparkling sequin clutch.

"Faisal?" She sounded as if she couldn't trust
that her eyes weren't deceiving her. As though
he were a figment of her imagination.

He knew that feeling all too well.

"You came," he said.

"I did."

"That means you received my note." He had asked her to come, leaving out everything of import that he wanted to tell her. Chiefly that he loved her, and he didn't want her flying from Istanbul without knowledge of how he'd grown from simply admiring her to adoring her completely.

"You look wonderful," he noted, his gaze roving her curvaceous figure appreciatively. He hadn't expected any less. Maryan could likely transform a paper bag into a couture gown in his eyes. She wore a dress of burgundy clouds, her bodice twinkling as if inlaid with the stars that were missing from the light-polluted night sky, and her jewelry challenging the effulgence of the sun itself. A goddess. That was what he was made to think when he looked at her. His reverence for her pairing with that glorious image.

"Zara liked this one best." Maryan slid her phone in her clutch and then pressed the purse with both hands to her center. "What are you doing out here?"

He could ask her the same. "I needed a breather. What about you?"

"Same," she uttered quickly.

A quietude closed over them, and then Faisal

grasped for his straws, a now-or-never mentality rearing up in his head.

"I thought you left."

She frowned lightly, the corners of her mouth drooping but her eyes dark and clear and reflecting the lighting around them. "Why would I leave?"

A few reasons popped into his mind, but he said, "I haven't given you a strong reason to come, that's why. I wouldn't have held it against you if you didn't stay."

She shrugged bare shoulders prettily. "Your message was vague... I was curious why you invited me after we decided that I wasn't coming."

"I never wanted you to stay away," Faisal said.

"You *didn't* say that," she snapped, and then breathing herself to a calm state, she continued, "I don't want to argue."

"Neither do I."

She lowered her clutch, looking far less defensive and far more curious. "Why did you invite me?"

"I wanted to see you."

Her clutch rose again, higher this time, above her heart.

"And I needed you to hear something," Faisal clarified. Taking courage that she wasn't running away or shutting him down, he relinquished the final traces of doubt about this approach and opened his heart to her.

"I tore this mansion apart looking for you. When I couldn't find you, I thought I'd lost you twice over. I felt double the anguish for my loss. Seriously, I thought the pain of losing you once was bad." He blew a shaky breath. "Then I saw you and it was like being given one last chance to set everything right.

"Because I realized as soon as you left my place that I shouldn't have let you leave us. That I was a fool to allow you to walk away. And I'd be a bigger fool not to tell you that I do care about you. Far more than I've let on. Vastly more than you'll likely believe.

"The thing is, I wasn't sure I could love you freely without mucking it up with my trust issues. But that's the thing: I *love* you."

Maryan was frightfully still, looking prettier than any painting by an old master, but appearing as though she'd checked out of his short speech.

Fear wormed its way into his blood and gouged his heart.

"Maryan?" he called out, taking a step closer to her.

She mirrored him, her eyes bigger, her mouth slightly open, her throat shivering with fast pulls of air and her chest heaving. She'd have scared him with concerns for her health if she didn't whisper, "What did you say?"

"I love you," he repeated.

"You do?"

He smiled fully, exquisite relief eradicating his worries. "Yeah," he drawled, laughing huskily, and saying it again for both their certainty, "I love you, Maryan."

He loved her.

All her hand-wringing and heart palpitations to make the same declaration, and he'd beat her to it.

*Does it matter who said it first? He loves me!*

"I'm not proposing marriage...*yet*," stressed Faisal, his eyes soft with the love he professed.

No, he was right not to propose. She didn't want to be married—at least not yet.

"I *am* asking you to give me a chance." He stepped closer, the gap between them sealing quickly when she met him halfway. "I want you to stay if you want, but if you need to be in America, I'll let you go. Whatever you desire, I'll try to be that for you."

"You want me to stay?" She was finding it hard to process all that he was telling her.

"I do. And not only because Zara wants you to stay, too."

Maryan blushed when his soft, sexy laughter washed over her.

"I thought I needed you as the nanny, and then you showed me that I could be Zara's father. Then I thought I needed you for a night. I haven't been wrong about much in my life."

She believed that. He was a billionaire. A fortunate entrepreneur, and a big-hearted one who was using his money for any good he could bring to the world. Somalia would be lucky to have him steering one of its first successful oil and gas businesses.

"But I've been wrong about this." He brushed a hand over her arm, taking that final step and bringing them as close as they'd been in the tangled sheets of his bed. Shivers broke out over her as his warm palm rubbed over her arm, up from her elbow to her shoulder, and back down to her wrist, his fingers interlocking around hers. "You're wearing the bracelet."

She looked between them where her other hand gripped her clutch, the mother-of-pearl bracelet he'd purchased for her from the Grand Bazaar shimmering like it knew it was being admired.

"It paired well with the dress," she said, laughing softly when he chuckled.

He lowered his head then, and Maryan understood what he was after, meeting him naturally. They kissed gently and faster than she would've wanted. Faisal explained, "We'll be seen. I don't want any media ruining this," before kissing her again, pecking her mouth with feathery brushes of his lips, breathing harsher with each short, fervent kiss. "I should stop. Before we get caught. But it's so hard."

He swallowed her laughter with a longer kiss.

When she went to grip his head, she remembered that his curls were gone. "You cut your hair."

"Do you hate it?"

She rubbed his shorter hair, the bristles tickling her hands, the sides shaved close while the top was darker and thicker. Shaking her head, she replied, "It's still very you." Then, feeling mischievous, Maryan teased, "I just won't have much to grip on to when you're—"

Faisal smacked a kiss on her lips, a warning growl heating her trembling mouth, "Don't make me regret having to stay at this party longer."

He hugged her then.

She held on to him tightly, unable to separate the sound of her heart from his.

When he drew back, his hands on her shoulders, his eyes darker, she sensed the direction of his thinking even before he voiced it.

"Do you…like me?" He didn't say *love*.

Maryan sighed. So, he'd noticed that she hadn't given him a response yet. There was a reason for it. He had gotten to say his piece.

*I need to say mine now.*

"I did want to run away at first," she confided quietly.

Faisal's brows pulled down, a frown storming over his darkly good looks and taking away the pleasure they'd just enjoyed. She knew he had to be wondering where she was going with this. But she'd had enough time to think this through, and she wasn't going to let fear hold her down any longer.

Cuddling his love close to her beating heart, she launched into this brave, new territory with him.

"Yesterday, in your garden, I told you that I was confirming flight scheduling with my aunt. The truth is… I've been wanting to stay."

She saw surprise flit over his face, but he didn't interrupt her.

"But then you didn't invite me to stay, and I got the sense that you might not want me to stick around."

"Which isn't true," he said roughly, shame supplanting his surprise. "I *should have* asked. I *should have* known what I felt for you wasn't leaving with you. I was a colossal idiot…"

"*You* were protecting yourself. I was, too. Otherwise I would've told you all of this sooner."

Faisal moved his hands from her arms to her hips, the comforting squeeze there meant to fan the flames of her courage. That wasn't sexual heat in his eyes, but a promise that he'd be there to catch her on the other side if she stumbled and fumbled her way through this important step.

"I've learned through my life that it's easier to accept the way things are, rather than yearn passionately for the things I wanted."

She swallowed, this part the hardest to say and hear aloud. "I wanted to stay with my family in Somalia. I wanted my parents to bring me home. I wanted my ex-boyfriend to understand why I couldn't be with him and not retaliate with petty theft. I wanted to stay with Zara for…well, forever. I love her, and it hurt to know that I'd likely never see her again."

Faisal framed her cheek with one of his big hands. "She loves you, too," he confirmed what she already knew.

"I *wanted* you. But I thought you didn't want me—*need me* beyond our physical chemistry."

"Now that you know I want *and* need you, too…"

She pushed up to kiss him quickly, sweetly, smiling against his lips, laughing away the last of her terrible unease.

"Tell me, Maryan."

So she did. "I love you, Faisal."

He kissed her until they were breathless, her lips sore and likely chapped, but her heart—her heart was with him. Nothing could pull her out of Faisal's arms, it felt like. Nuzzling noses, she imagined their night could be spent out there, just the two of them.

Rudely, his phone vibrated and forced them apart briefly.

It was only when he had his phone in hand that she remembered what she'd been up to before she noticed him behind her.

"Faisal, there's something else…"

She blanched when he looked up at her from his glowing phone screen, one eyebrow rising slowly, a stunned expression slackening his jaw.

"I *might* have posted some pictures," she began with a shy, nervous smile. And when he didn't respond, she backed away.

Faster than she could get away, his arm hooked around her waist, and he hauled her in, looking unfazed when she yelped.

"I can see that," he rumbled sexily. "You finally tagged me."

"I'm sorry!"

She expected to do more groveling, but he sealed their lips in a hot, lingering kiss, before whispering, "For what? Remember it was my idea from the beginning."

She did remember that first day in Istanbul; Faisal tried to get her to tag him in the photos of them together. She hadn't wanted her friends to bug him…but now they were bugging them, and she couldn't separate it from her happiness.

"Although your grand gesture has mine beat."

She snorted. "It might have ended badly, though." If he didn't love her.

Thinking the same, Faisal said, "It didn't."

He hugged her tighter to his side and angled his phone so they could both see the comments that were beginning to trickle in, and fast. Support from her friends and followers, and from his. Everyone either wanted to know the nitty-gritty details or wanted to know when the wedding was happening. The photo was of them on the rooftop restaurant, their love for each other glowing from their faces even then.

"I'll have to explain to Salma."

"Worried?" Maryan asked, knowing that Zara's mother wasn't in love with Faisal, and she wouldn't stand between them. Yet she sympathized with any concern Faisal might have. Especially as there was someone else who would have to know about them. "We'll have to tell Zara as well."

He touched his lips to her temple. "Afraid of what she'll think?"

"A little. Aren't you?"

Faisal stared into her eyes, and she knew that he had her full, unwavering trust whatever he said. "It's only been a day and she misses you terribly. She loves you. Still, I won't pretend that it won't require adjusting on all our parts, but I know she'll be happy for us."

Trusting him, Maryan leaned in as his arm settled over her shoulders and read more comments until Faisal shut off his phone.

"Since you're staying in Istanbul for longer now—"

"Am I staying longer?" she teased.

"If you *choose* to extend your stay, I'll happily charter a flight for you whenever you wish to leave for America."

She laughed, kissing his cheek, finding his lips, and nearly losing track of her thoughts before she pulled back to mock gasp. "A plane? I knew a billionaire was a catch." She giggled when his mouth brushed the heated tip of her ear.

"Is that a 'yes'?"

"I'll have to call my aunt and uncle to let them know about us. Though I can't stay long. I still have to help them…"

Faisal kissed her sweetly and touched their foreheads together. "Whenever you want to go, you let me know. Distance won't be a problem."

She believed him. And not only because he had a private jet at his disposal. She didn't think her heart could feel so dangerously full before, but he surprised her with better news.

"Guess now is a good time to tell you that someone else will be happy for us."

"Who?"

"My family. My mom especially. Fair warning in advance, she might talk you into marrying me."

She snorted a laugh.

"Seriously though, Zara and I will be leaving to visit them in a few days. I want you to come with us."

He didn't need to twist her arm. Nervous though she was, meeting his family would be exciting and meaningful.

"And maybe one day we'll get to visit yours?" Faisal hedged.

"Actually...after I left you yesterday, I got to thinking that I should visit them soon. Likely before the end of the year. There's a lot I need to say to my parents. A bunch of healing that needs to be done."

He pulled her in and bussed her cheek. "That's big of you."

She blushed, feeling like she'd never react any differently when he praised her so warmly. And she wasn't any less bashful when broaching the final topic they had to discuss.

"What happens after I leave Istanbul?" She hadn't settled on where to live, mostly as this was still fresh to her. They'd only just confessed their love to each other.

Faisal seemed to have thoughts on it, though. With one of his winning smiles, he hugged her closer, turned her to the magical Bosporus, and vowed, "No matter where we end up, here in Turkey, or America, or Somalia, I'll love you always."

"I'll always love you, too."

"Even when I'm running late?" he laughed.

Grinning, she promised, "Even then."

* * * * *

*If you enjoyed this story,*
*check out this other great read*
*from Hana Sheik.*

Second Chance to Wear His Ring

*Available now!*